"AN ASTUTE COMEDY OF LITERARY MANNERS."
—*The New Yorker*

"He is occasionally likened to Proust, but, as Evelyn Waugh once noted, Powell is much funnier.... Now, happily—and surprisingly—a new 'Powell,' as his readers put it, has surfaced ... a brief, lively, slightly acidic account of the undoing of an aging literary not-quite-lion ... a satisfying entertainment."
—*The Cleveland Plain Dealer*

"Anthony Powell is over the jumps again, an elegant master of the course.... Shadbold is a wonderful comic character."
—*The Boston Globe*

"His fiction ... continues to offer as much pleasure as that of the great nineteenth century English novelists."—*The Guardian*

"A DELIGHTFULLY WITTY LITERARY DIVERSION."
—*Publishers Weekly*

ANTHONY POWELL, one of the greatest twentieth century English novelists and stylists, is the author of the wonderful series of twelve comic novels, *A Dance to the Music of Time,* and four elegant volumes of memoirs. He is also the author of six other novels, a biography of John Aubrey, and two plays. In 1984 he received the Bennett Award "in recognition of his distinguished achievement in the art of the novel."

O, How the Wheel Becomes It!

A NOVEL

Anthony Powell

A PLUME BOOK

NEW AMERICAN LIBRARY

NEW YORK

For Hilary

Library of Congress Cataloging in Publication Data

Powell, Anthony, 1905–
  O, how the wheel becomes it!

  I. Title.
PR6031.07402 1985   823'.912   85-10527
ISBN 0-452-25756-5

PLUME TRADEMARK REG. U.S. PAT. OFF. AND FOREIGN COUNTRIES
REG. TRADEMARK—MARCA REGISTRADA
HECHO EN HARRISONBURG, VA., U.S.A.

SIGNET, SIGNET CLASSIC, MENTOR, PLUME, MERIDIAN and NAL
BOOKS are published by New American Library, 1633 Broadway, New York,
New York 10019.

First Plume Printing, November, 1985

1 2 3 4 5 6 7 8 9

PRINTED IN THE UNITED STATES OF AMERICA

OPHELIA You must sing *A-down a-down*, and you *call him a-down-a*. O, how the wheel becomes it! It is the false steward, that stole his master's daughter.

Hamlet. IV.5

O, How the Wheel Becomes It!

1

In one or other of G. F. H. Shadbold's two published note-
books, *Beyond Narcissus* and *Reticences of Thersites*, a short
entry appears as to the likelihood of Ophelia's enigmatic
cry: "O, how the wheel becomes it!" referring to the chorus
or burden "a-down, a-down" in the ballad quoted by her a
moment before, the aptness she sees in the refrain. Shadbold follows up this comment on archaic usage of the word
with the reflection: "But as to the first wheelwright's
wheel, only a step was required from invention of that disc
rolling on its own axis as an aid to transport for man to
develop those potentialities into the even graver menace to
his kind of the roulette-board."

Simon Beverly-Baines, an old enemy, observed of this
aphorism that the wheel's threat to the human race would
have been yet more dire had Shadbold himself driven a car
(which like quite a few writers he abstained from attempting), and, by temperament unaddicted to games of chance,
Shadbold himself stood in little or no risk from the wheel's
hazards in the context of the green-baize table. As usual
Beverly-Baines (whose obituary Shadbold managed to
write for one of the national papers) was not altogether

just. Shadbold had more than once staked the price of a ticket in the lottery of life's more intimate relationships (where taking things all in all his luck had been nothing to complain of), while even Beverly-Baines would have had to concede that Shadbold, during a career devoted to the craft of letters, had shown willingness—even recklessness so far as his own capabilities were in question—which signified no fear of an occasional gamble. Doubtless one could also argue (as implied by extension of the image) that the wheel often symbolizes the manner in which nobody can tell where things are going to lead, nor to what purpose they may not be twisted.

To recall Shadbold's *oeuvre*, since memories are short: in extreme youth he had produced the slimmest of slim volumes of verse, *Unweeded Gardens*, of which in maturity he spoke lightly, saying the title betokened that Housman had not yet been weeded from Eliot. How he managed to get this collection of juvenilia into print no one knew. It remained one of the unsolved mysteries of contemporary literature. Probably the publisher, one of the optimists in a predominantly pessimistic profession, had hoped for great things from a Shadbold novel. If so, the hope stayed unfulfilled.

"Everyone these days writes a novel about their school experiences," Shadbold told his friends. "I'm changing the pattern and writing a play." He did. The play was called *Irregular Conjugation*. During his early schoolmastering phase it was performed by Shadbold's pupils, and led to the sack from that particular school. After he had achieved a certain degree of fame *Irregular Conjugation* was printed in a limited edition on handmade paper by The Forte et Dure

2

Press, an item likely to be tagged "Does not turn up often," and flatteringly priced in booksellers' catalogues.

Two novels did appear in due course: *Trip The Pert Fairies* ("Milton dethroned, *Comus* endures," Shadbold excused the title), mostly conversations in the Peacock tradition; then *Thumbs*, described in reviews as "experimental." Neither did much in the way of sales, *Thumbs* especially meagre commercially speaking, though both were tolerably received by the critics. Bavaria was then somewhat in the mode, but *Bavarian Swan Song* (Wittelsbachs, Lola Montez, Oberammergau) was remaindered. A short study of one of the Cavalier poets (Denham, Suckling, possibly Lovelace), commissioned by an inexperienced publisher for a series of minor poets, was taxed with gross inaccuracy by a reviewer (its sole one) in the *Times Literary Supplement* but in language so immoderate that Shadbold, on the whole successfully, was able to laugh off the notice as a piece of academic pedantry. There was a fair amount of collected journalism of one kind or another, and, quite late in the day when Shadbold had already made some name for himself, the two selections of extracts and apophthegms.

Notwithstanding the comparative leanness of this output Shadbold was not to be dismissed as a lightweight, a mere hack. He had worked hard reviewing other people's books up hill and down dale, tirelessly displayed himself on the media and elsewhere in every variety of lecture, quiz, panel-game (at the last of which, endowed with an exceedingly reliable memory supported by wide reading, he was unusually proficient), also always prepared to offer views on marginally political subjects for which he was less accredited by instinct. Insofar as the cliché can be used

3

without irony he had become a respected literary voice. Indeed long before he died Shadbold himself was fond of playfully asserting that had he lived in Japan—where age as such is revered—he would by then be receiving positive veneration. He may well have been right.

When the second war came Shadbold, in his middle thirties, had time to consider the position without undue bustle. He early expressed the conviction, a tenable one, that he would be a liability in the armed forces, and by returning intermittently to schoolmastering, possibly undertaking a short spell of quasi-governmental employment in a rural area towards the close of hostilities, contrived on the whole to steer a course through wartime dangers and inconveniences without undue personal affliction, reducing to a minimum interference with a preferred manner of life. Shadbold never for a moment claimed to have brought off from lofty motive this comparative immunity.

The chief casualty of Shadbold's war was his first marriage, rumoured to have been in a fragile state for some years before. His wife, a young actress called Kay Conroy, who specialized in *gamine* roles, departed into a ferment of theatrical activities aimed at entertaining troops, and never returned. A divorce was quietly arranged without excess of bad feeling on either side.

Finding that so far as girls were concerned he was not having too bad a time Shadbold took no immediate steps to remarry; a condition he maintained for perhaps twenty years or more. After the war, the period from which his name began to grow steadily as a critic, he set about consolidating a sound professional reputation. In doing that he was sufficiently successful to find himself in a position to buy a cottage—neither too small nor too far from London—in an agreeably unbuilt-up area within range of the sea.

He remarried in the 1960s.

Prudence, the second Mrs. Shadbold, much younger than her husband (her third), was also unencumbered by children, although—like the preferred mother-in-law of the anecdote—she possessed a lot of experience. Red-haired, handsome, serious in demeanour, she disseminated the impression that she was presenting a rather valuable Literary Prize from a daïs in a room full of fellow authors. She herself wrote bestselling detective stories under the pen-name of Proserpine Gunning. Shadbold may even have met her in the first instance through an often expressed admiration for the *roman policier* as a genre. Certainly he was an *aficionado* (his own term) of the detective novel. At a stage when his earning potential was inevitably a falling market owing to increased age, the Shadbold domestic budget must have substantially benefited from the annual Proserpine Gunning hardback, which appeared regularly, and never let its readers down.

2

In the late 1920s—to use the phraseology of carbon-dating give or take a hundred years—Cedric Winterwade also had a novel published, his first and only one. Winterwade and Shadbold may have been at school together, legend persisting (though neither went that way in later life) that Shadbold had seduced, or at least attempted to seduce, the slightly younger and appreciably better-looking Winterwade. Undoubtedly they had overlapped as undergraduates, by which time friendship, though continuing, had probably become platonic enough.

On coming down from their university Shadbold, a schoolmaster's son, set out on a teaching career (classics and history) at the school where *Irregular Conjugation* had been performed by the boys with untoward consequences. Winterwade, also following paternal employment, went into the City (a stockbroker's office). Neither found his job sympathetic, but Winterwade, though he never seems to have done more than earn a bare living, remained where he was. His calling gave him at least a vicarious concern with those lucky or unlucky throws to be associated with Shadbold's metaphorical wheel. This aspect may have held Winterwade's attention more than even he himself was fully aware. There was later some recorded evidence of that.

The teaching profession conspicuously lacked any such fortuitous excitements, and Shadbold decided to get out. He gravitated (with the intention of writing a book when time allowed) to the precarious slopes of literary journalism. There he found himself possessed of that happy knack attaching to some persons—even a few writers—of extracting money from unexpected sources and obscure enterprises; not large sums as a rule, nevertheless useful in making two ends meet in Shadbold's early days of free lancing.

Shadbold and Winterwade remained in close touch after coming to work in London where Winterwade, in spite of a daily round broken only by Contango Day, retained the intellectual leanings of his undergraduate period. In that field Winterwade was accustomed to be treated as rather a poor relation by Shadbold, who nevertheless at times discussed with his friend literary matters that were of interest to both of them. In London too, although professionally they operated in such very different spheres, Winterwade's intermittent contacts with the arts caused him to be invited—at least occasionally taken—to the large, promiscuous, usually pretty rackety parties since become something of a legend of that day. The glimpses each caught of the other at these gatherings never developed into competition over the same girls.

In this last respect Shadbold cruised about with average good fortune (no more), the incident of Bunty Meadows illustrating a typical adventure, exceptional only in being a brief cause of anxiety. Shadbold and Bunty Meadows, a girl of genial approach to life, went to bed together after a

7

party at which both of them had drunk a good deal. Shadbold was only too well aware that going to bed with Bunty Meadows was nothing to boast about, so that when a month or two later disaster threatened, it was brought home to him abruptly that he had behaved on that evening with imprudence.

In short Bunty Meadows came along to Shadbold with the news that she thought she was going to have a baby, and wanted a comparatively large sum to arrange matters in a manner convenient to herself. Shadbold (having just spent the modest advance on *Trip The Pert Fairies*, soon due for publication) had no money to spare at that particular moment, nor was he by any means convinced of his own responsibility for the condition in which Bunty Meadows supposed herself. While the crisis lasted there was a considerable to-do, clouding with worry Shadbold's satisfaction in the publication of his first novel. Then Bunty Meadows came to see him again to say that some other (unnamed) friend of hers had offered to fork out the required sum if necessary.

Shadbold, who never set eyes on Bunty Meadows again, though she thoughtfully rang him up to announce that the whole business had been a false alarm, was thoroughly shaken up by this episode. In fact he had scarcely recovered his composure when a short time later Winterwade disturbed him again by revealing that a publisher had just accepted his, Winterwade's, first novel. Shadbold was sufficiently taken aback by the fact that his friend had been capable of writing a novel, much less a publishable one. While offering congratulations he had to admit to himself that his nerves were more than a trifle jarred by the information. Winterwade's novel was called *The Welsons of Omdurman Terrace*.

When this unlooked-for work appeared Shadbold found with relief that *The Welsons of Omdurman Terrace* offered no serious competition with the sort of writing he judged himself to produce. The story, set at the turn of the century, portrayed a lower-middle-class London family of a kind that Winterwade could at best have known only second-hand. Some critics, indeed, claimed that howlers had been committed in descriptions of day-to-day life at that social level, additionally marred by anachronistic dialogue. So far as there could be said to exist a coherent plot the hero was let down by his friend over a girl, who went off with the friend just at the moment when the hero was about to become engaged to her. A dreadful breeziness of tone was interspersed with extravagant sentimentalities.

Shadbold, who detected faint echoes of H. G. Wells, Arnold Bennett, even at times George Gissing, privately considered Winterwade's approach not only old-fashioned, derivative, facetious, pedestrian, but imbued with every vulgarity of mannerism and thought possible to accommodate within fictional form. His own ambitions, as indicated above, showing a bias towards modernity and perfectionism, caused him to feel shocked as well as gratified by the unmitigated awfulness of his friend's novel, which he had no means of knowing would be Winterwade's last. Although unwilling to give much weight to his own respect for Winterwade's mind, conversations with him had at least often brought out unexpected viewpoints.

Winterwade himself did not seem in the least worried by unfavourable animadversions on the part of the more highbrow reviewers regarding his literary style, and it was true that the less fastidious book-columns, if devoting space to *The Welsons* at all, inclined towards praise. In this and other respects people found Winterwade an inscrutable fellow. His aim may in fact have been not in the least inscrutable—that is to say, simply to bring in some ready cash as quickly as possible by what he judged might be the synthetic construction of an instant bestseller. Indeed it looked at one moment as if Winterwade's goal might be attained, *The Welsons of Omdurman Terrace* in fact take wing. Then some move in the political game (probably too early for Hitler, prime demolisher of contemporary authors' hopes) dealt a blow from which sales never recovered. Nonetheless even the limited success *The Welsons* achieved for a few weeks after publication established Winterwade for the moment on the map of a not very distinguished literary continent, his name, anyway in the eyes of the lower-grade reviewers, being marked there in more prominent letters than Shadbold's own.

If Shadbold felt resentment as to Winterwade's transient pre-eminence—in the light of subsequent events it is unlikely he did not—he showed no outward sign. On the contrary, so far from rebuking his friend for lack of *avant garde* principles, his review of the novel commended an attempt, even if not a wholly successful one, to break away from the constricted world of intellectuals and their tedious love affairs. Shadbold's manner of expressing approbation might have been thought a shade condescending by veterans of the critical battlefield, but his words stopped well the right side of risking offence. At that moment Winterwade and Shadbold still presented every appearance

10

of being on the best of terms with each other. Inwardly, however, Shadbold may have made up his mind already that friendship with Winterwade might prove a professional handicap. Certainly after the publication of *The Welsons of Omdurman Terrace* the two of them drifted steadily apart.

3

Back in that palaeolithic age Shadbold fell in love with Isolde Upjohn. This passion was, emotionally speaking, something incalculably different from romps with girls like Bunty Meadows. Isolde Upjohn personified the current fashion in *le sex-appeal*: figure of infinite slimness; next to no breasts; permanent expression of pained surprise; smattering of talk about books and pictures. So far as she might be said to follow externally any gainful employment hers was the engaging one of model. She modelled clothes for fashion papers (rather than naked for artists), and, having at one point in early life attended an art-school, augmented such earnings by herself at least once executing decorations illustrating an article in the margin of the fashion paper whose advertisement pages displayed her own photograph advocating *haute couture*. There was in fact no inherent difference in subject-matter between photographs and drawings (the last scarcely to be designated otherwise than cute), both depicting Isolde Upjohn herself wearing whatever garments or lack of garments might be required to enliven the letterpress or sell the clothes.

Although not inordinately luxurious (had she been so

Shadbold among others would not have remained long within her orbit) Isolde Upjohn found such sources of income as mentioned above insufficient to keep body and soul together within the bracket she had ordained for herself: thereby necessitating existence in the background of some figure better equipped financially than the average young man to be found hanging about her Chelsea flat. Such young men were unlikely to be in a position to pay the flat's rent regularly, even if good for an occasional dinner at The Eiffel Tower or bottle of gin to ameliorate an unannounced visit.

Who "kept" Isolde Upjohn was not generally known. Shadbold *et al.* took for granted that the anonymous benefactor belonged to a generation senior to their own. They lived in hope that even if the affluent lover was not (as optimistically supposed by some of the rival and increasingly embittered aspirants) utterly decrepit and preternaturally hideous, a girl might, if only momentarily, yield to her own caprices, take a fancy to a hard-up suitor.

In the belief that Isolde Upjohn would prove no exception to this time-honoured tradition, Shadbold, replenished by all the ardour of hopeless love, would when sufficiently in pocket ask her to dine with him at some restaurant well outside his normal sphere of expenditure, the dream always in the back of his mind that tonight could be the night when Fortune, in the guise of Isolde Upjohn, might smile on his hopes. Isolde Upjohn's flat teemed with such young men, because whenever she met a personable male she asked him to come and see her. They always did.

That was just what happened one evening when Shadbold and Winterwade were walking together eastwards down the King's Road on the way to catch a bus and dine in Soho, as in those days there was nowhere admissible to eat in Chelsea. They came upon Isolde Upjohn about to enter the house where she had a top-floor flat. As she already knew Shadbold she invited them in to talk to her while she changed for her own dinner engagement that night. Shadbold, who would have been only too delighted to receive such a summons had he been alone, was not particularly pleased this should happen when accompanied by Winterwade, to whom—since as remarked earlier they inhabited rather different worlds—he had never mentioned Isolde Upjohn; nor for that matter Bunty Meadows. He lived in perpetual fear of fresh rivals, though in fact one more or less would have made little or no difference in their daunting array at Isolde Upjohn's court. At the same time the intrusion of a personal friend (Winterwade had not yet revealed himself as fellow author) would have been peculiarly unwelcome in that capacity.

As things turned out Winterwade showed no signs whatever of falling for Isolde Upjohn that evening, while she herself displayed no more than a routine demeanour of insatiable man-eating that was at the same time essentially unsusceptible. As she was already late for her dinner engagement the visit was not a prolonged one. On leaving the flat Isolde Upjohn was found a taxi, Shadbold and Winterwade catching the bus they had been seeking when the encounter had taken place.

"Had you ever heard of her?" asked Shadbold.

"The name seemed faintly familiar. She's not bad-looking, is she?"

"She's all right," said Shadbold. "I take her out occasionally."

14

"Rather too much like the cover of *Vogue*?"

"When you're having dinner with her tête-à-tête one sometimes gets the impression of having a cut-out from a *Vogue* cover propped up in the chair in front of you."

Shadbold thought it safer not to appear too enthusiastic even to Winterwade, of whose exploits in the amatory field he had in fact no very high opinion. Winterwade laughed. The subject of Isolde Upjohn did not crop up again in the course of the evening, which was chiefly devoted to discussion of Shadbold's plans for his next novel.

Perhaps a year or two after that, before circumstances might otherwise have convinced Shadbold that he was wasting both time and money—neither in unlimited supply for one making his way in the literary world—in pursuing this fruitless aspiration, Isolde Upjohn herself brusquely terminated the relationship (such as it was) by getting married, and going to live abroad. Her husband, said to be an oil executive on leave in London, unknown to Shadbold or any of Shadbold's acquaintances—unknown probably to the clandestine springhead from which Isolde Upjohn's quarterly rent derived—bore her away over the sea to Arabia, Persia, whatever enchanted land gushed forth his oil.

Shadbold, who had his romantic side in those days, was for the moment greatly cast down by this final loss of Isolde Upjohn, notwithstanding that love for her when on the spot had been at times little less than torment. Even several decades later, when he ran across an ad-man who, once frequenter of the Isolde Upjohn flat, had hazarded the opinion that she was dead, the pang Shadbold experienced, in part conscious self-pity for his own lost youth, was by no means entirely dissociated from thought of the passion he had once been capable of feeling.

The drifting apart of Shadbold and Winterwade had become complete when Winterwade married a very pretty
girl, a doctor's daughter, who had worked for a time at the
BBC. By then Shadbold was possibly not even invited to
the wedding, but he may have seen photographs of Winterwade's bride and been piqued by her good looks. Physical
removal had disembarrassed him of love for Isolde Upjohn,
and, no doubt stimulated to competition by the Winterwade marriage, he proposed to the *gamine* actress Kay Conroy, and was accepted.

Shadbold's wartime experiences, the dissolution of this
first marriage, have been briefly touched on. Winterwade,
either because he possessed a more adventurous philosophy
of life, was influenced by romanticism of another sort, or
supposed that he would be conscripted sooner or later anyway and might just as well get in on the ground floor,
contrived to join the army, a commitment from which age
and some minor physical disability (flat feet or something
of the sort) could at least momentarily have absolved him.
Shadbold, who had plenty to occupy him in satisfactory
manipulation of his own wartime affairs, may or may not
have known of Winterwade's military involvement at this
early stage. He did, however, hear not long before things
ended that Winterwade had lost his life; in what circumstances Shadbold never bothered to ascertain.

4

So far as Shadbold was concerned the whole unfortunate course of subsequent events began in the bar of the Garrick Club, where he was drinking with Jason Price, who had unexpectedly invited him to luncheon. Price, titular whizz-kid in Shadbold's publishers—if in the highest sense of the term a writer who had not produced a book for over a quarter of a century may be said to possess a publisher—was a young man who liked to carry the firm's banner into hitherto unexplored regions, especially those of the past. There was a deliberate touch of neo-Teddy-Boyism about the way he dressed, including a Lord Kitchener moustache, which expressed a nostalgia for mythical eras like The Nineties or The Twenties (the second after Price had to some extent exhausted the possibilities of the first), decades (as he himself put it) of intoxicating women and intoxicated men dancing a pavan through lost kingdoms of Cockayne. In his professional role he had sometimes been successful in reviving forgotten names from such epochs.

Price's association with Shadbold was in fact not so much professionally in the administrative field of publishing as off duty (more or less) in the role of drinking companion at the The Garrick bar on Shadbold's fairly regular visits to London. At these meetings Shadbold would sometimes recall legends of his own period (or those heard by him of earlier ones) to satisfy what had become with Price almost an obsession. In consequence of this relationship the most convincing account of the events leading up to G. F. H. Shadbold's end was chiefly owed to Jason Price, though some of the more exotic aspects of the saga may have done more credit to Price's powers of imagination than documentary accuracy of memory. He had, for example, no compunction in reporting conversations and states of mind with which he could not possibly have been directly familiar. On this occasion in the bar Price reverted to a discussion with Shadbold that had taken place between them a year or two before.

"You remember, Shad, some little time ago I asked your opinion about republishing a forgotten novel called *The Welsons of Omdurman Terrace*, author Cedric Winterwade, and you advised against?"

"I recall something of the sort."

"You said Winterwade had virtually copied it all from other novels, not to mention getting a lot of stuff wrong anyway, and that even if it had sold a bit in its day nobody would be interested now."

"If I uttered those words they still represent what I think. I knew the man, as I probably told you at the time. Poor old Cedric couldn't write novels for toffee—not if you offered him the Rokeby Venus to screw—though it always seemed to me that he had certain gifts of observation and wit, which might have been put to advantage by a man of keener instinct. *The Welsons* was altogether too contrived. I

18

said a good word for it when the book appeared for friend-ship's sake, and because I thought Cedric had a kind of talent deep down. But it wasn't for novel-writing. It wasn't for money-making either. He was in the City, and never did more than scrape along. In short he was a nice but rather ineffectual chap. That's why no one remembers him."

"You think Winterwade might have written something one day?"

"Who can tell? If he hadn't been mad enough to go into the army and get killed. Though I don't know what he could have done."

"Those whom the sods love—didn't Aubrey Beardsley write in one of his letters?"

"The sods didn't particularly love Cedric," said Shad-bold.

He wondered for a moment whether he was being got at about the alleged school incident, then decided Price was very unlikely to have heard the legend, still less refer to it.

"Nor the girls particularly either for that matter," Shad-bold added. "Until he met his wife. Besides he wasn't all that young when he died, though I suppose you might say young for a writer. Cedric was always rather well behaved. He never even drank very much."

"Perhaps that was part of the trouble," said Price. "Ernest Dowson remarked that absinthe makes the tart grow fonder—I mustn't impose The Nineties on you, Shad, as I know they bore you. But I'm interested in what you've been saying about Winterwade. I'll tell you the rest over lunch."

Shadbold's suspicions had already been aroused by Price's invitation. He felt something ominous in the publishing line might be in the air. It could hardly be a question of pulping stock as all his own works had been long out of print.

"Shad," said Price, when they were settled at the table, "do you know what happened to Cedric Winterwade's widow?"

"No idea—not even whether alive or dead. You aren't still agonizing over *The Welsons of Omdurman Terrace*, are you, Jason? I'm certain it won't sell."

"No, no. In the end I quite agreed with you that the novel was too bad to republish. I just wondered if you knew about the widow. If not, I can tell you. When Winterwade died she remarried."

"I'm not surprised. She looked a very pretty girl from pictures, and also from what I've heard of her. We never met. I wonder whether she'd have stayed with Cedric. By the time he married I hadn't seen him for ages."

It occurred to Shadbold that he might be wise to soft-pedal earlier friendship with Winterwade.

"Not long after Cedric Winterwade's death his widow married an Australian who'd been over here with the Australian forces. It must have been just after the war. The former Mrs. Winterwade accompanied her husband back to Melbourne, taking the Winterwade children with her."

"How many?"

"Two, I think. It's immaterial. She and her second husband died within a few months of each other about a year ago."

"Jason, why am I being told all this?"

"Wait a moment. Winterwade's son is a journalist. On *The Melbourne Age*, I believe. Anyway he was going through the family effects after the funerals of his mother and stepfather when he came across what appeared to be a diary kept by his father as a young man, indeed until just before his death, I think."

"I see."

For some reason this news made Shadbold feel uneasy. He regretted having admitted to have been once a close friend of Winterwade's in the past.

"Winterwade *fils* knew nothing of its existence. Possibly his mother didn't either. It was mixed up with a lot of miscellaneous papers of very varying importance brought out with her to Australia and never properly sorted out."

"And the younger Winterwade wants to publish this diary?"

"More or less. It's not as easy as all that."

"Libel?"

Shadbold saw that from his own point of view that aspect must be emphasized at once.

"For one thing. As to how much libel may be an objection is at present not clear. In fact much is not at all clear. Winterwade had a vile handwriting, used abbreviations all the time, and concealed the names of the individuals he wrote about at all fully by symbols."

"You've got the manuscript?"

"It's been the rounds of the publishers, and now fetched up with me."

Shadbold saw how things were shaping.

"What do you think of its prospects yourself?"

"That's the point, Shad. Winterwade *fils* is not particularly interested in his father, and is reported to find *The Welsons of Omdurman Terrace* unreadable. That period in London is naturally unknown to him. The war even more so, nor has he the least inclination to decipher a lot of

21

hieroglyphics. On the other hand he would like to make a bit of money out of the thing if any money is to be made. That is what I gather from the intermediary."

"The son's not over here himself?"

"He sent the ms. to another Australian journalist in London. Asked him to do the best he could. If no go, send it back."

"What's your general opinion?"

"Can't tell without some preliminary editing. That's needed before even a serviceable typescript can be made. The transcriber would have to take decisions sentence by sentence as to meaning, while getting the material on to paper in an even roughly intelligible form."

"How long?"

"I judge it might be published in one fairly bulky volume."

"And you want me to have a look at it?"

"That was indeed the idea, Shad. Perhaps do the editing yourself."

In principle Shadbold was not averse from tasks of that kind, if made worthwhile. He was, however, sufficiently experienced to guess, were Winterwade's Diary anything like what Price outlined, that a good deal of effort would be needed even to read the ms., much less edit the contents; probably more exertion than at Shadbold's age he would be prepared to volunteer in the ordinary way, certainly unless pretty well paid. In general he felt no keenness for the sort of editing that demanded conscious scholarship. At the same time the side of him that took pleasure in the mechanics of detective stories (though he had never attempted to write one himself) included a taste for solving puzzles. The cryptographic aspect of the manuscript provided a certain appeal rather than the reverse.

All these considerations were small ones compared with the curiosity he felt, which over-rode any doubts that might make the Diary seem untempting to tackle. However much trouble was threatened the prospect of retracing some of the ground he and Winterwade had covered together was too inviting for Shadbold to resist whatever the conditions; nor was he wholly indifferent to having set before him in this chance manner a record that would no doubt chronicle Winterwade's own findings about his sole literary success, now sufficiently lost in oblivion to be safely referred to in relatively generous terms. In the event, after a bit of haggling over the fee (negotiations which Price was capable of handling in as tough a manner as Shadbold), it was agreed that a report should be made, the possibility of editing borne in mind. What happened after that was principally filtered through Jason Price's later sometimes not wholly consistent versions of the story.

5

Winterwade's combined illegibility and secretiveness turned out even more disordered and undiscoverable than Shadbold's worst apprehensions had anticipated. He saw easily enough now why publishers had quickly passed the Diary from hand to hand. Nonetheless sufficient entries were, so to speak, *en clair* for him to grasp at once that Price was right to suppose the Diary had commercial possibilities, while from Shadbold's personal point of view he was in the highest degree gratified that it should have come his way. With a little trouble many of the passages were clearly going to yield matter of absorbing interest to himself. The question of whether or not the stuff would be saleable as a book could be decided later. There was no doubt whatever that Winterwade's latent talent consisted in keeping a diary.

The best method of grappling with the problem of decipherment in a manner to give quickest satisfaction to himself, however laborious, seemed to be to type out some of the material relating to the years when Shadbold had been seeing a good deal of Winterwade. If the Diary was attacked in this manner Shadbold hoped that at the same time he would be able to elicit the meaning of at least some of the secret symbols, as day to day, week by week, Winterwade's life was unfolded. This process would be helped by his own memories of persons and happenings of the period. On the whole the Diary did not record daily events with close attention, sometimes missing weeks, even months, then concentrating on some perhaps trivial incident that had caught the diarist's attention.

Shadbold did not take long to identify the mark used in some of the earlier passages (dating rather scrappily from university days) to signify himself. He was relieved to find that such references were on the whole comparatively flattering. Shadbold was praised for intelligence and wit, though not for reliability or social ease. On balance Shadbold did not too much resent that conclusion. He would have awarded Winterwade a similar proportion of contrasted good and bad marks for this and that had he himself been the diarist. So far as what Winterwade named social ineptitudes were concerned Shadbold's subsequent career satisfied him that his friend had simply been a poor judge of such matters. If no worse were to come, the Diary would present an acceptable picture. Personal remarks about himself could be suitably dealt with in editing, were that to take place. He had not yet made up his mind whether editing would be desirable, or better to pass on an undeniably onerous task to someone else, while perhaps at the same time arranging to retain certain controls over what was published.

Several symbols evidently represented girls. Shadbold was not able to mark down all of these. Rather to his surprise, even faint irritation, he noted that Winterwade too had been to bed with Bunty Meadows; indeed a year or more before he himself was to share that intimacy. This had taken place on one of Winterwade's comparatively rare excursions into that particular *demi-monde*, and clearly antedated the troublesome incident in a manner to disclaim any possibility of Winterwade being in the running for co-blame. Shadbold had to admit from individual experience the incident was described with both skill and veracity. Winterwade's failing as a novelist seemed to fall away from his writing when it came to chronicling personal insights.

One symbol, formed rather like a small crown, seemed to represent a woman with whom Winterwade had been deeply in love. Against its first appearance were scrawled some lines in the margin:

> *I am the queen of Samothrace,*
> *God, making roses, made my face.*

Shadbold, whose not very high opinion of Winterwade's literary abilities permitted his friend little or no critical acumen where poetry was concerned, allowed himself a touch of supercilious amusement at someone who had to fall back on Swinburne to express the emotion of passion. At the same time he felt decided interest in discovering who this girl might be, as she seemed to fit in with none of the other women of whatever kind who figured in the Diary, nor with what little Shadbold knew of Winterwade's love-life from conversations with him. Shadbold had spoken without much respect of Winterwade's status as a lover when discussing that with Jason Price. The Diary showed that at least some re-estimate might have to be made.

Once or twice the inconceivable suspicion assailed Shadbold that the Queen of Samothrace reigning in Winterwade's heart might be Isolde Upjohn. Remembering the occasion when the two of them had come across her in the King's Road, together gone up to the flat, he dismissed the idea, so plainly had it been a first meeting for Winterwade. Then he came on an account of that particular evening.

Now he found that the far from desired introduction of Winterwade that night had been by no means an initial encounter, though it may have been Winterwade's first visit to Isolde Upjohn's flat. Where or how they had originally met Shadbold did not for the moment bother to ascertain. That could be done later. The point was that both had been accomplices in the deception. Shadbold was puzzled and annoyed by this deliberate hoodwinking of himself, even more so by phrases used by Winterwade in recording his friend's "pitiful gaucheries in conducting an abject love." Far worse was to come. A few pages later something really devastating to Shadbold's self-esteem was revealed. The shock was a truly severe one. It appeared that Isolde Upjohn had agreed to be taken by Winterwade to Paris for a weekend. To add an unthought-of horror to that project she had apparently suggested the trip herself.

The rending pain of the stab experienced on decoding the entry in the Diary which recorded this proposal was a surprise even to Shadbold himself. He had not called Isolde Upjohn to mind for years, would have supposed such mortification unthinkable in the circumstances. The fact—if fact it was for he could scarcely believe such a thing—of having put forward the idea of going to Paris herself was not to be borne.

Up to that stage of what was recorded of Winterwade's

love there had at least been for Shadbold a certain relish in feeling that Winterwade had been suffering the same agonies, the same lack of success, as himself, even if the smoke-screen raised by the pair of them continued to rankle. Where those very emotions were concerned he had to recognize that they were described by Winterwade with consummate skill. There was no doubt whatever that the latent ability had been talent as a natural diarist. The jar to Shadbold's nerves was therefore made more acute not only by the unexpectedness of the revelation in the light of his own acceptance of Winterwade's indifference, but also from the course of entries charting unappeasable longings, reduction to the same hopeless despair, that had consumed Shadbold himself. Winterwade's progress hitherto had been superior only in taking a clandestine form (even if thereby suggesting a keener interest on Isolde Upjohn's part), all this notwithstanding the diarist's recorded contempt for Shadbold's technique of seduction: the last a minor matter in the light of the inconceivable that had come about.

After having to swallow the fact that the visit to Paris had been put forward by Isolde Upjohn herself Shadbold felt all but knocked out with rage and envy. Then he pulled himself together. There was still vestige of hope. Grappling feverishly with the Diary's illegibilities and abbreviations he looked ahead into its pages to see if by any lucky chance the promised adventure could finally have fallen through. It was possible from what he knew of Winterwade's financial arrangements that sufficient funds might not have been available for the trip at the last moment. Another hope was that Isolde Upjohn—at the best of times given to changing her mind about minor matters—would suddenly decide that she did not want to go to Paris after all.

Shadbold knew by now from what he had read of the Diary that any such disappointment would be chronicled with the ironic detachment in which Winterwade as a diarist excelled. Pray God, thought Shadbold (in Jason Price's narrative), that gift may be needed to the uttermost. Such hopes were vain. Winterwade accompanied Isolde Upjohn to Paris. The trip took place during a period in his own life when Shadbold seemed to remember he had been in particularly low spirits.

The whole episode—which occupied at least a dozen pages of the Diary—was set out in Winterwade's most accomplished vein. The experience had in fact been a good deal less than idyllic. Winterwade himself was the first to recognize that. Life's way—anyway Love's way—always possessed lights and shadows, the shadows as often as not predominating. Winterwade emphasized that fact with amused resignation. Shadbold found philosophic appreciation of this truth, Winterwade's pitiless transcription of the episode's ups and downs, obnoxious in the extreme. If Winterwade had indulged in transports of bogus delight Shadbold could more easily have dismissed the descriptions as fictitious. An uncompromising realism was even more offensive to a literary critic of his own acknowledged standing.

An uneasy atmosphere had apparently hung over the trip from the very beginning, Winterwade never fully understanding why this hitherto utterly unforeseen bounty had been vouchsafed to him. In fact it looked very much as if Isolde Upjohn had manoeuvred the whole affair for her own purposes in order to be in Paris at that precise moment, the presence of a companion preferable, and cheaper, than going by herself. Possibly (thought Shadbold), though direct evidence of anything of the sort was lacking, the visit had something to do with making sure of the man who subsequently married her. According to the Diary she had disappeared for at least two stretches of several hours, saying she wanted to shop. On return to the hotel she had been pale, tired, thoroughly out of sorts.

The venue itself offered additional provocation, even if a lesser one in comparison with the revelation that the coupling had occurred at all. Its scene had been l'Hôtel Bouguereau et des Artistes to which Shadbold himself had rather magisterially introduced Winterwade as ideal resort for the impecunious but sophisticated and cultured. It was a small establishment on the *rive gauche* where Shadbold had once quite by chance spent a night, ever afterwards boasting of its discovery. Now he tried to assuage this minor item of resentment with the recollection that, however cheap and clean accommodation at The Bouguereau, the beds were uncommonly hard.

As a matter of fact that thought brought little relief because Winterwade did not pretend that being in bed with Isolde Upjohn had been in the least a triumph of sexual felicity. On the contrary she had revealed herself (Winterwade's phrase) as "contumaciously frigid and uncooperative." He wrote cool-headedly about that too, recording the condition as no more than expected (Shadbold had to agree he would have supposed the same himself), nonetheless recording the achievement over the weekend of three or four orgasms. The registration of even one of these would have been sufficient unbearably to exacerbate Shadbold. Winterwade tabulated each in detail, at the close of his account of the Paris episode returning once more to *The Masque of Queen Bersabe*:

> *In Shushan toward Ecbatane*
> *I wrought my joys with tears and pain!*

By then Shadbold was too dispirited to sneer afresh at Winterwade's old-fashioned taste in poetry. He knew pretty well what Winterwade must have felt when he quoted those lines. That did not reduce his own indignation; nor did the indications, plain enough, that Winterwade's initial success with Isolde Upjohn, such as it was, had never been followed up. The Diary recorded her going off on one of her "holidays" almost immediately after return to London, an action quickly succeeded by announcement of the marriage, final departure from London.

Shadbold's imagination stopped short of picturing anything more displeasing to himself—even equally displeasing—that might emerge from the remaining considerable bulk of the Diary, which ran to (he did not bother to reckon) many hundreds more pages, though he saw that, in spite of stringent regulations against keeping a diary when under arms, Winterwade had evidently continued to do so in the army until shortly before his death, altogether ignoring that prohibition, or at least writing up experiences when on leave. By now, broadly speaking, Shadbold's attitude towards the war was that even if it had unquestionably taken place (which he never went so far as to deny) the whole episode had been grossly exaggerated by those with a vested interest in making capital out of wartime experiences. The crowning disfigurement of the Diary was for life in the army to be depicted. In any case to know with absolute certainty what else was included was impossible unless he took the same trouble in unravelling illegibilities and obscurities that had already been spent in following a single thread which happened to be of interest to himself for personal reasons. Any further effort would be abhorrent. He mentally released himself from any obligation that might be owed to Price, for that matter to Winterwade, by deciding to report that he was so certain the Diary was not worth publishing he had proceeded with it only to a limited extent, would therefore be prepared to accept a somewhat reduced fee.

6

Jason Price, dishing the whole matter up for the thousandth time, used to reiterate his own astonishment at receiving from Shadbold such a virulent report. He said: "It made *De Profundis* look like a Collins." For a moment Price wondered whether the manuscript ought to be set aside for further consideration by himself or some other professional reader. A less damning dismissal would have been in some ways more reassuring. There was something fishy about Shadbold's violent feelings. Then, as he was very busy at that moment, Shadbold after all was the highest authority he knew on the subject of Winterwade, there was undoubtedly a lot of trouble involved in reading the script, Price saw little point in pursuing matters further. It was not impossible that Shadbold, too indolent to do the work properly, had heartily condemned as the easiest way out. So be it. The decision was in principle adverse. Whatever the cause, tedium was implied. Price decided he would not bother to get an opinion from an additional source. He returned the manuscript whence it came, and forgot about the diarist.

How impartially Shadbold would have assessed matters

had Isolde Upjohn made no appearance among the Diary's entries must remain problematic. The prospect of post-humous celebrity thrust in wholly unexpected manner on a former friend, one not only regarded at the time as a very moderate performer but by then deemed safely defunct in all literary connexion, could in any case have proved highly dissatisfying. Shadbold was sufficiently versed in such matters to feel assured that, even were Winterwade's Diary not to sell immediately in large quantities, its merits were of a kind—properly presented and edited—to attract a great deal of critical attention. Who could say if in the future there was not danger of the Winterwade Diary taking its place as a minor classic, becoming a household word? That would have been a painful thought had it been necessary to ponder.

In thus attempting to suppress publication Shadbold was freely rejecting any prestige he might himself have acquired in appearing as virtual discoverer of the Diary, annotating its obscurities with exact knowledge as un-disputed authority on Winterwade's early years. Shadbold must have recognized he was to that extent making a sacri-fice. He ignored such potential loss without reluctance. Isolde Upjohn rankled too much. She might or might not be deceased; Winterwade's spell in bed with her may have been a frost; since those days Shadbold himself had been married twice, experienced a reasonable measure of love affairs; the fact remained that so far as Isolde Upjohn was concerned Winterwade had got there, Shadbold had not. Alive or dead, frigid or passionate, paid for or free, scarcely mattered. Winterwade not Shadbold had taken her to Paris.

Her name could, it was true, remain unidentified in a

34

published version of the Diary, a symbol—as in the manuscript—conceivably deducible to one or two veterans of
the epoch with long memories and personal knowledge, no
more than that; a band decreasing in number, expanding
in amnesia and incoherence. A symbol would also offer
solution beyond the risk of libel (were Isolde Upjohn still
en vie), or touchy relations (if any) left behind. Nonetheless, so far as Shadbold was in question, the disaster had
taken place. He himself would always flinch under the
sting. That was enough. Almost anyone—he could think
of no competitor—would have been more forgivable than
Winterwade. If the name of the diarist's mistress remained
concealed in the event of publication the truth would still
gnaw at Shadbold's vitals as long as he lived. Even were the
passage (one of the most striking) to be omitted, Shadbold
himself would still know. The draught was too bitter to
swallow, especially on top of seeing Winterwade's name
once more in every paper. The true abomination was
within Shadbold himself. One whole facet of memory had
been dislocated. The prearranged myth held in his mind
comprehended an image of Isolde Upjohn uncontaminated
by any recorded physical connexion with a man known to
him personally, least of all Winterwade. The misty figure
or figures in the background paying the rent were no more
than phantasmagoria of an unpleasant dream. The desecra-
tion of myth, on the other hand, was something not to be
condoned in any circumstance.

7

In later life, though his days were spent conventionally
enough, G. F. H. Shadbold had become mildly hippy in
outward appearance, growing a beard, wearing at desultory
length such hair as remained to him, pottering about in
odd garments. So far as work was in question minor assign-
ments came in and went out with fair regularity, bringing
a steady if restricted revenue. The Winterwade Diary, had
not unforeseen impediments precluded the acceptance of
editorship, would have constituted a typical professional
employment, one solider, more rewarding, than the usual
run of things. Shadbold spent some of his time gardening,
of which he possessed sufficient acquaintance for an occasional horticultural article embellished with usually fairly
recondite literary quotations. Such a field indicated a desirable breadth of culture in a critic. Prudence Shadbold was
always working on a new Proserpine Gunning detective
story. Of the current book she had revealed no more to her
husband than that the plot involved a redbrick university.
The two cats, Lord Jim and Gentleman Brown, maintained their mutual running warfare, which if one aban-
doned the other would take up. Mrs. Trout came in three

or four days a week. Routines at the cottage were as usual. On the surface all was humdrum enough.

Prudence Shadbold, belonging to a considerably younger generation than her husband, was unfamiliar with the name Cedric Winterwade when mentioned as that of a defunct contemporary who had kept a diary, nor had she ever heard of *The Welsons of Omdurman Terrace*. She showed no interest whatever in diary, novel, or report to Jason Price. The Proserpine Gunning books were handled by another firm, and she knew of Price only as a young man in her husband's publishers with whom he drank from time to time when in London. The return of the Diary brought about such enlargements as Shadbold chose to give her. They took place at luncheon.

"Oh, Pros, could you post a parcel for me if you're going near the town this afternoon? As I told you, Jason Price sent a manuscript to me to read and I want to return it to him."

Prudence Shadbold preferred to be styled by the diminutive of her pen-name, which emphasized status as writer rather than wife. It fitted in well with her husband being known almost universally as Shad.

"Any good?"

"No."

"A novel?"

"The Diary of a contemporary of mine."

"I'm never keen on diaries as reading matter, though they're sometimes useful in developing a plot."

"The man who kept this one was rather a shit."

By that time Shadbold had made up his mind that to take Isolde Upjohn to Paris had been a disgraceful act on Winterwade's part; an enormity aggravated by its sequel

that she had proved frigid ("little short of rape, the bugger," thought Shadbold savagely), not to speak of a supposed friend committing so squalid and brutal an assault in
an old crony's favourite Left Bank hotel (its very name revealed only out of pure kindness of heart to a novice), sur-
rounded by the faded but dignified and serene *belle époque*
fitments of The Bouguereau.

"That ought to have made the Diary more amusing."

Shadbold roused himself from a reverie of hatred.

"What ought?"

"The fact that the diarist was a shit."

"He was the wrong sort of shit."

"You always say all your contemporaries were shits."

"Most of them were. Still are, the majority of those who
contrive to hang on in this Vale of Tears. What on earth are
we eating?"

"Pork chops."

"What's happened to them?"

"Mine's all right."

"Mine's playing hell with my metabolism."

"What's wrong with it?"

"Consistency like one of The Dry Salvages."

Shadbold felt thoroughly aggrieved. The Diary had
ruined his appetite for the day. He continued to find himself meditating more than convenient on his action in writing as he had to Price; in fact to such an extent that he was
forced to call to mind one of his own maxims in *Beyond
Narcissus*: "Guilt should be treated as an impudent intruder
in the house of the artist, not an ailing guest whose caprices are indulged through familiarity so extended that
unease has almost become friendship." On a number of
past occasions when he might have behaved a shade equiv-

ocally that principle had served him with very fair success. He saw no reason why its robustly remedial doctrine should not continue to sustain his declining years. Nonetheless, in spite of repeating the words aloud to himself, he was still undeniably conscious of the weight on his mind of what could be regarded by others as shabby behaviour towards a fellow writer, much less old friend.

Such twinges (caused by the *super-ego* or the *anima*, for the moment he could not remember which) Shadbold attributed more immediately to a general weakening of the nervous system that accompanies increased age, the declensions of time notoriously causing atrophy of resistance in certain areas, notably failure of the will. Reflecting regretfully on his younger days—when, fitter than now for life's struggle, guilt had scarcely troubled him at all—he braced himself to expel the whole matter from his mind. He could not help feeling gratified to recall the fact that Simon Beverly-Baines was no more; then the train of thought began to raise doubts about the obituary of Beverly-Baines he had himself written. Those were easier to dismiss simply by allowing imagination to dwell on how Beverly-Baines would have behaved had anything so unfortunate happened as his hearing of Shadbold's condemnation of Winterwade's Diary. Even so the very vision of Beverly-Baines at such a moment suggested more than usual disharmony in the air. The thought that less strong terms regarding the Diary might have been wise would not be dismissed, yet less strong terms would have been to increase risk of another publisher's reader making a favourable recommendation. Did that matter? Would he have been better advised to have steered clear of the whole wretched Winterwade affair?

8

Throughout his career Shadbold had always made a practice of accepting invitations to speak at literary societies, college clubs, reunion dinners, in fact gatherings of whatever kind, if requested to address them. He enjoyed public speaking, at which in his own manner he was quite a finished performer, the anecdotes kept for such occasions (carefully graded) being less than virgin, but never terminating without a trustworthy punch-line. He accompanied these talks with a good deal of theatrical "business," personal quirks that hardly needed exaggeration as he grew older, assisted by a few minor eccentricities of dress, also improved rather than diminished by clothes decaying with their owner. The whole performance had been brought to a high degree of perfection in timing by recurrent use.

As age crept on, Shadbold had perforce to cut down a little on these jaunts, which he regarded as an integral part of shoring up his own market, nevertheless managing to attend a good proportion of them still, even if days were over of going almost anywhere for expenses and a free meal. Among public appearances of that kind The Outsiders, an engagement due soon after the return of the

Winterwade Diary, was no run-of-the-mill overture to be accepted or refused at whim. The Outsiders was an undergraduate club of predominantly literary flavour at one of the newer universities and, in case other inducements were insufficient, on this particular occasion an available fund had been raided for the purpose of paying for a talk by Shadbold, raising the honorarium to a figure a shade less risible than usual.

That was by no means the sole reason for accepting The Outsiders' invitation. It was launched through Horace Grigham. Grigham, an EngLit don at the university in question, was not only patron of the Society, but—more inherently of consequence—one of the former husbands of Prudence Shadbold. The Shadbolds had indeed both stayed with the Grighams on earlier visits without either of them being under obligation to speak. That possibility had however been ventilated as something desirable in the future.

Although Shadbold did not like Grigham he preferred for a variety of reasons—some shared by his wife—to keep in with him. Shadbold's antipathy was due not so much to natural undercurrents of jealousy as because Grigham's face irritated him. Grigham also wore a beard that Shadbold felt let the side down. The Newgate frill of the Victorians, it extended into a narrow furry ruff, framing features all a trifle too large. Bald, intense, stooping, with protruding eyes and huge rimless spectacles, Grigham had chosen for his second or third attempt at marriage a wife in vivid contrast with Prudence (now) Shadbold. Janice Grigham's almost deliberately unornamental appearance was in no way indemnified by amiability of manner, a formidably severe demeanour forbidding all commonplaces of smalltalk. She would listen unmoved to Prudence Shadbold's prize-awarding speeches,

41

saying she must slip away to practise the bassoon or oboe (Shadbold forgot which), her sole hobby.

Prudence Shadbold having more than once hinted in public that being in bed with Horace Grigham was by no means plain sailing, some credited Janice Grigham with unexpected knowledge of and exceptional dexterity at esoteric techniques which amply compensated her husband for what might be looked on by some men as superficial imperfections. Others for their part held that Grigham sought no more than as absolute a change as he could find from marriage with Prudence Shadbold; being prepared to go to any lengths in order that the aim should be achieved.

The Outsiders was therefore a burden, insofar that it was a burden, needful to take up, and, whatever his personal prejudices about the Grighams themselves and their household, Shadbold was aware of actually looking forward to a spell in new surroundings even for a single night; transference to a scene where the ghost of Winterwade was unlikely to walk. There were no difficulties about the talk. He did not intend to write anything *ad hoc*. He would give his routine lecture (now a thought dusty, but continuing to go down well with young audiences), "Woodbine or Concubine: the Poet's Dilemma." Grigham, who liked to flirt with the latest fashions in literary criticism—anyway nearly the latest—would heckle, but having to listen to Grigham's reedy voice after the talk was all part of the package-deal in earning a small sum of money, getting one's name round among the young, together with in this case the exceptional bonus of shaking off Winterwade guilt. Besides Shadbold felt himself, intellectually speaking, to tower over Grigham, who might say what he chose.

The post-talk supper given by the committee of The

Outsiders was eaten in a small restaurant situated on the far side of the University from the Grighams' flat, a fact noted with a certain apprehension by Shadbold, who had hoped to end the evening as early as possible without enduring too long a drive in Grigham's unluxurious car before getting back to bed. Chez Mithradates, he mentally named the restaurant after sampling menu and wine-list on which *Pommes Orwell* and *Vin Pipi de Singes* respectively might well have figured. Shadbold, resigned to such things, remained in sufficiently good humour to appreciate the looks, especially the doe-like eyes, of a young female member of the committee who sat on one side of him. The girl was not only familiar with *Reticences of Thersites* (quoting fragmentarily at least one of the epigrams), but showed signs of being additionally well disposed in order to pique Grigham, who undoubtedly had an eye on her. Indeed all was going as well as might reasonably be expected when, as a matter of routine, Grigham put a stop to general conversation about halfway through the meal by embarking on what was evidently going to be a critical attack on the lecture, something for which Shadbold had been perfectly prepared.

"Those Jacobethan poets you touched on tonight, Shad. Don't you ever feel yourself required to reinterpret? Structural determinants underlying their lines of projection? I'm sure systematic semantics would attract you with your particular shape of mind."

Shadbold felt inclined to tell Grigham to keep off the grass where his, Shadbold's, mind was concerned, but dismissed the temptation.

"Naturally reinterpretation of any writer, poetry or prose, is always a possibility, Horace."

"In the light of contemporary needs, I mean."

"Whatever may be contemporary needs as you call them —and I would not deny some such may exist—there is all the same no harm in being aware of traditional attitudes. I think even you would concede that, Horace."

Shadbold began to prepare himself for carrying war into the enemy's country were that necessary, though not immediately unless pressed. In any case he was pretty sure Grigham was unlikely to have listened with sufficient attention during the talk to be able to persist in being annoying by display of close knowledge of what had been said. Acceptance or refutation was therefore available as convenient, whatever form of arguing the toss Grigham might choose to adopt. Shadbold, as emphasized earlier, had an excellent memory, one of his most formidable weapons, and in any case this was no more than shadow-boxing.

"I wasn't questioning the limited validity of what you put forward, Shad, not at all events so far as it goes, even linguistic validity to some extent. No, I'm sure your assertible stipulations are valid enough, anyway most of them. It was just that one's understanding is compelled towards the matrix in either poetry or prose. The social matrix mainly—though of course one keeps an eye on the political matrix too—of the pictorial medium. Dialectical determinants, you know."

Shadbold, not for the first time, felt thankful to be too old ever to have run the risk of being numbered among Grigham's unhappy students, condemned daily to martyrdom which was for himself but a single night's infliction, painful as that might be, for which he was being paid rather than paying, albeit inadequately. His immediate problem was to extract one more substantial glass of the dubious vintage without at the same time unduly protracting the evening, notwithstanding that he could just feel the warmth of the girl's leg next to his own. The best tactic seemed temporarily to humour Grigham by pretending to take him seriously; if that failed become obstreperous, and insist on being piloted back to the flat without delay.

"In your own words, Horace, a fact is only a term in inter-subjective reciprocal changes of sign, so naturally where poets, especially Jacobethan poets, are concerned . . ."

Shadbold spoke the sentence with a dying fall. He knew Grigham must have culled the formula from some book or periodical devoted to such obfuscations—probably got it wrong at that—and would be unable to follow up in argument whatever shreds to be called a train of thought might be drifting through his mind. Having fielded this globule of Grigham jargon from some former conversation Shadbold hoped the small offering of flattery implied by its retention would be held sufficiently in his favour to be looked on by Grigham himself as a profitable note on which to terminate the evening's proceedings. If that came to nothing, less obliging methods would have to be put into operation. Grigham, however, was clearly moving towards another purpose, some obscure destination of his own on which he was intent.

"Let's leave poetry for the moment, Shad."

"Willingly."

"What I'm going to say needs a little explanation."

The moment had come to tease Grigham into sub-jection.

"Before we abandon poetry, Horace, I must tell that I was tempted to quote *The Sow-gelder's Song* in my talk. Then I thought one never knows with that sort of audience. You remember it of course?"

"Just mention the provenance."

"*The Beggar's Bush.*"

"Middleton, Dekker? I confess I am uncertain."

"Fletcher actually, with perhaps a touch of Massinger. I'm surprised the play's slipped your memory. Surely you recall that Pepys saw *The Beggar's Bush* several times?"

"What about the song?"

"It was just what you were saying regarding the matrix made me think of it again. Let me quote it now:

> *Take her, and hug her,*
> > *And turn her, and tug her,*
> *And turn her again, boy, again;*
> > *Then if she mumble*
> *Or if her tail tumble,*
> > *Kiss her amain, boy, amain!*
>
> *Do thy endeavour*
> > *To take off her fever;*
> *Then her disease no longer will reign*
> > *If nothing will serve her,*
> *Then thus to preserve her,*
> > *Swinge her amain, boy, amain!*
>
> *Give her cold jelly*
> > *To take in her belly,*
> *And once a day swinge her again.*
> > *If she stands all these pains*
> *Then knock out her brains,*
> > *Her disease will no longer remain.*"

Shadbold's neighbour giggled appreciatively, and suffered her knee to press gently. Grigham, so far from being antagonized by this brisk change of tempo, challenge to his own professional equipment as a scholar, pounced on the carefree tone of the Sow-gelder as vehicle for what he himself wished to talk about.

"Excellent, excellent. The whole spirit of the song brings us suitably enough to what I wanted to ask your views about, Shad. I mean in the broader sense the Sow-gelder's sentiments remind one of the style we associate with The Twenties. Actually not the particular book to which I'm going to refer, but we will go into that. I must begin by telling you that I have been making something of a survey into the insightful fiction of fifty or more years ago."

Shadbold stiffened. He preferred both *Trip The Pert Fairies* and *Thumbs* to remain decently undisturbed in their respective sepulchres; certainly not to be even partially disinterred after all these years of peace by the dissection of Grigham's literary anatomy class for students of English. He had not thought about his own early books when deciding to bait Grigham.

"Ah?"

"Not always easy to discover."

"So I should suppose."

Whether or not Grigham at that moment recalled the fact that The Outsiders' guest of the evening had himself written a couple of novels in distant days was doubtful so intent was he on his own purpose. That possibility never came to light, one way or the other, during Grigham's more exact specification of his recent literary fumblings.

"I've been browsing among the novels of The Twenties and early Thirties, usually searching in vain for sociological frameworks, not devoting myself so much to novels that might be categorized as satirical or experimental . . ."

Grigham paused for a moment, probably with the object of making clear that for better or worse he did not propose to discuss Shadbold's two contributions to novel-writing at that date.

"Both types are to be found extensively in fictional work of the period—whimsy, too, marriage to foxes and monkeys, copulations with witches and the Devil—no, it's the old realistic tradition struggling on that I'm concerning myself with. There I have found signs of something significant—at least one—mutilated, one might say axiomatically, but meaningful as sociological analysis."

"I see."

Shadbold allowed his mind to wander. The great thing was that his own books were not to be dredged up. From time to time the girl's throbbing leg advanced or retired while he tried to think of another method of harassing Grigham.

"You follow me?"

"In essentials, Horace."

"I'd like to have your opinion on a particular writer of those years if you've ever heard of him."

"Go ahead. I didn't by any means know or read them all."

None too delicately Shadbold suppressed a yawn.

"I wonder whether in your early days you came across a novel called *The Welsons of Omdurman Terrace* by one Cedric Winterwade?"

The question was so unexpected that Shadbold could think of no adequate comment. Grigham seemed not to expect immediate recognition of so obscure a title.

"I am not in the least interested in the personalities of

writers as such, but if you knew Winterwade by any chance you may have read his book."

"Years ago I knew him."

"And read his novel?"

"Without remembering much about it."

"Excellent from my point of view that you should have done even that. What was your judgement? Can you recall?"

"I am hardly qualified to give one at this distance of time. More especially in the critical terms you prefer, Horace."

"You would agree attempts at realism in the manner of Bennett?"

"Bennett-and-water."

"But touches of Wells."

"The Gissing-end of Wells."

"Other less worthy models?"

"No doubt."

"I see we are in general agreement. Towards the end of the book these influences tail off."

"What was left of Wells, I wonder, when the Gissing had to stop—or of Winterwade for that matter?"

Grigham frowned.

"No one is more aware than myself that the author is merely a nodal bond, yet Winterwade's production is an individual one, however in many respects banal and derivative. His novel attracts me for study. In one sense unexpected culture-codes and utterance-types are to be seen after the pressures mentioned have been allowed for. That in spite of reiterant weaknesses in meaning-determining emphasis."

"So I should guess."

"I suspect that a critical examination of *The Welsons of Omdurman Terrace* would rather neatly reveal certain theories of my own."

"You would be the best judge of that. I should be doubtful of expecting too much. I wonder whether there's anything left in that bottle, Horace?"

Grigham poured the dregs of the enigmatic fluid into Shadbold's glass.

"Winterwade was killed in the war, I think?"

"Stone dead. His book too."

"I sense your reactions are unfavourable, Shad?"

"On the whole, yes."

"I shall have to think things over."

Shadbold deftly changed the subject.

"I hear Prudence is coming to stay with you and Janice in the near future."

"As I'm sure Prudence has already told you, she wants a campus background for the next Proserpine Gunning. The scene is laid in a university. We are flatteringly to provide the backdrop, though Prudence assures me that resemblances in the story are to be purely geographical. Prudence hinted that some of the characters. . . ."

Grigham, sniggering, breathed into Shadbold's ear the name of another redbrick foundation in a different part of the country, which was apparently to provide some of the human interest in the story.

"I knew it was to be a campus novel. No more than that."

Grigham shook his head a little sadly.

"Although we are ever delighted to see Prudence the aim of her visit struck me as a little old-fashioned, if one could ever call Prudence old-fashioned. Nowadays emphasis in the dectective novel is laid no longer on the pure mechanics of movement and discovery—maps of the district, plans of country houses, all that paraphernalia beloved of the past."

Shadbold was not going to risk Grigham telling Prudence when she came to stay that he himself had sat down under this sort of criticism of her writing, something which would undoubtedly cause strife. Nor was he thus prepared to take dictation as to how detective stories should be written from a mere academic, much less of his wife's books from a former husband.

"Don't you consider accuracy of presentation to be welcomed, Horace?"

"Social comment, if only implicit, is the preoccupation of the better detective writers of today. You must surely agree the bourgeois world of Sherlock Holmes and Dr. Watson is no more with us, Shad?"

"You forget, Horace, that in *The Priory School Adventure*—which I concede betrays snobbish overtones in the disappearance of a duke's son—the murdered German master's name is Heidegger, no doubt father or uncle of the Existentialist philosopher Martin Heidegger, from which ontological hint the story should surely be judged?"

Grigham laughed irritably. Shadbold had not finished with him.

"Not only that, but the maths master is referred to as Mr. Aveling."

"I fail to see the significance."

"Clearly Edward Aveling. A little-known interlude in the life of the lover of Karl Marx's daughter. You will remember the poor girl thought Aveling was going to marry her, but Aveling found a richer wife for himself. No doubt

Holmes had a file on Aveling—perhaps on Marx too under M, next to Moriarty and Moran. Holmes's political awareness often comes through in the stories, though naturally he concealed it for his own reasons."

Grigham allowed himself another ice-age smile. Shadbold was past caring whether or not umbrage was taken by Grigham or anybody else present at the table. He had supped his fill of The Outsiders and their hospitality. All he wanted was sleep. He consolidated his position with a final broadside.

"Compare the repressed homosexuality of Holmes and Watson with that germinating kleptomania in Raffles. So far as Prudence is concerned, she may intend to anatomize some of the social problems posed by you academics. That might not be too difficult."

Shadbold wondered from Grigham's face whether he could have gone too far. Possibly he had. Grigham was certainly enraged by this slur on his trade. Aware somehow that in speaking of Winterwade he had laid a finger on a raw spot he saw the best riposte was to return to that former subject, rather than speak up for himself and his fellows.

"Let's get back to Winterwade for a moment, the man whose novel we were talking about earlier. I am struck by the total oblivion into which the book has fallen. There is a certain challenge there. Can you suggest anyone else of your own generation, Shad, who might remember *The Welsons of Omdurman Terrace* better than yourself? You're one of the few friends I possess of your years."

Grigham always liked to draw attention to the fact that he was a good deal younger than Shadbold. Winterwade's book gave an unrivalled opportunity for dwelling on the gap.

"I wonder, for example, whether Winterwade left any unpublished works. He died young."

"Uncover his novel. Mine eyes don't dazzle. Most of the people who knew Winterwade are probably dead by now. I shall expire myself in this restaurant, Horace, unless we go home soon."

"You're looking rather tired, Mr. Shadbold," said the girl.

She withdrew her leg finally, but gave her doe-like side-glance.

"I have a delicate constitution," said Shadbold. "I should have been granted an aegrotat in the university of life."

Goodbyes were said to the committee of The Outsiders, who had themselves become a little restive under the later stages of Grigham's critical commentary. Shadbold fitted himself somehow into the horrible car. As they clattered away to the furthermost borders of the town he was conscious of sinking ever deeper into the mire of a campaign directed towards the suppression of Cedric Winterwade's memory.

9

"How was it this time?"

"Penitential. I woke in the night with a racking thirst, and could find nothing to drink out of but an ash-tray."

"You fill me with dread."

"Do you really have to go?"

"Without more exact knowledge of up-to-date university buildings and teaching routines I can't work out the time sequences of the murder, which depends on a matter of minutes. There may also be computer methods now in use I should enquire into."

"That struck Horace as very old-fashioned for a contemporary detective novelist."

"Horace doesn't know what he's talking about."

"Agreed Horace would be better lecturing at Broadmoor or Rampton as a participating inmate, but that's what he said."

"What were his actual words?"

"That ground-plans and time-tables are out of date these days. The world of Sherlock Holmes is over. All that. The modern detective sets out with the implicit suggestion that he is a social worker investigating a social problem, not just getting back a rich woman's jewels, or foiling a secret society of which a merchant banker was once a member and is in consequence receiving three avocado stones enclosed when his dividend warrants arrive."

"Of course a modern detective is clued up about sociology. Horace must be more of a fool than I supposed if he thinks I don't know that."

"I tried to make clear that we are all only too well aware of changes in that field."

"Besides there's plenty of sociological criticism in *Culture-code of Samphire*."

"What's that?"

"The title of the new Proserpine Gunning."

"Good God, culture-codes are one of the things Horace is always rambling on about. There's nothing in the book about hermeneutics, I hope. That's another of Horace's obsessions. I thought you said that neither Horace nor any of his colleagues were going to figure in the story? This sounds Horace to the life. Dead-ringer."

"Horace no doubt pontificates about such matters, but I know him well enough to be certain that's showing off. I've been told on the best authority that he's far from expert, just mugged up some of the simple textbooks. Besides Horace isn't queer, at least hasn't been for a long time."

"What's being queer got to do with it?"

"Part of the social angle."

"In what way?"

"A disadvantaged boy is exploited by élitist academics, then murders one of them. As there's been a death-grapple intrigue in the university about a well-endowed professorial chair the murder looks as if it might have been committed by one of the Faculty."

"Is the murderee deprived too? One or two of Horace's colleagues struck me as just that."

"Another suspect is a student who has stolen an EngLit examination paper."

"Can't you cut out the culture-code stuff? Horace is bound to think it's meant for him. Besides so many people must feel like murdering him. Although the most pacific of men, I did myself. That alone will make Horace recognizable. I hope Janice doesn't come into the book too— setting F. R. Leavis to wind and percussion, for instance?"

"Certainly not."

"No mention of wind instruments."

"Nothing in the least like Janice and her French horn. Did she play it while you were there?"

"A few notes—Oh may she join the choir inaudible."

"The point is all resemblances will be ironed out when the book is revised."

"Then you admit resemblances exist?"

"Don't worry. After all I was married to Horace. I know what is and is not safe to write about him."

"And don't get caught up in some student really having cribbed the answers recently, and been implicated. One reads about that in the paper. They're always doing it."

"I'll make sure about that."

"It's Horace I'm really worried about. I didn't know there was any question of his ever having homosexual leanings, when younger, with a face such as his. Your story sounds otherwise much too much like him and his present crowd. Tell me more details about it."

"The Professor who gets murdered is more like Shaun Truefitt, for instance, with a touch of Reggie Stalling."

"Why does the boyfriend do it?"

"Because the don gets married."

"As a cover-up?"

"Some high-minded reason I haven't worked out yet. The high-mindedness makes it more difficult to identify with Horace. There'll be another sociological angle there."

"The voice that breathed o'er Auden/That earliest wedding day?"

"Something of the kind. The boy is rough stuff with intellectual yearnings, not an uncommon type I'm told."

"And Horace's prototype seduces him linguistically?"

"If you care to put it that way. When the marriage takes place the boy goes downhill."

"Gives up hermeneutics? Throws away his Wittgenstein? What does the title refer to?"

"*King Lear* of course. One that gathers samphire, dreadful trade. The boy gets nicknamed Samphire by his more highbrow clients because he's dreadful trade."

"I hope the boy isn't someone we all know too. But surely after what you've told me you could work out the sequences just by taking a little thought? Do you really have to trek off to the Grighams'? I don't recommend it."

"Safer to walk the ground. I'll just have to put up with Horace and Janice for forty-eight hours. It will make it easier to omit any chance stuff that might resemble them or their household if it's all fresh in my mind."

Shadbold did not wish to run any risk of libel, nor to persuade his wife into a course of action that might prejudice the accustomed high standard of credibility and fast-moving narrative of a Proserpine Gunning story, thereby risking decrease of sales. He did not as a rule mind being left alone for a day or two. By now his feelings towards Horace Grigham were scarcely at all coloured by jealousy.

The reason for this opposition to Prudence Shadbold's absence was simply fear of being marooned with Winterwade all day as well as all night. He returned to the subject some time later when she told him that she had received by post from Janice Grigham a pair of socks that he had left behind on his stay there.

"Janice also asked me to bring back the Lévi-Strauss book you borrowed."

"Borrowed? Horace forced the bloody book on me when I said that as far as I was concerned Lévi-Strauss was only revered because he invented jeans. But look here, when you go to the Grighams' the week after next do make sure you sketch the plot of *Samphire* fairly fully. It would be safer. You don't want it all to come as too much of a shock. Make absolutely certain they don't think the book is about themselves and all their friends."

"You exaggerate. I'll do something of the sort if you like. But it's next week I'm going, not the week after next."

"The Grighams think it's the week after next."

"No, they don't. Janice mentioned the date in her letter."

"But if it's next week you'll miss Rod Cubbage."

"I know."

"Why on earth choose that moment?"

"I want to go in the middle of the week."

"Why not the weekend?"

"It's weekly routines I hope to check on. Besides the Grighams said they didn't particularly want me at a weekend. I don't think they particularly want me anyway, so I had to take what was on offer. Anyway it's you Cubbage is doing a programme about, not me."

"Even so, he'll expect you to be there too. It will look odd if you're not present."

"No, it won't. If I appear on TV I'd rather have a programme to myself. In any case I don't want to be programmed by Cubbage. It gives me a pain in the guts even to watch his face on the screen."

"Cubbage will want to hear about your work, Pros. What shall I say?"

"Point dramatically to the Proserpine Gunnings in the bookcase."

"The public would rather look at you as more decorative."

"The public will have to wait. You can explain my mission. That will show how *sérieuse* I am as an artist. An indication of the high status of the detective story, something you are always advocating. Have you finished with the Lévi-Strauss? If so why not give it to me now, so that I shan't forget to take it with me?"

Shadbold made a gesture expressing utter despair.

"Finished with it? Yes, I have finished with it. Just about. Christ, what a book. In fact *Christ in the House of Lévi-Strauss*, one of Veronese's lesser-known masterpieces."

10

The expectation in the offing of a programme about himself and his work had been far from displeasing to Shadbold, more especially one in the current series by Rod Cubbage. Nothing of the kind had taken place for some years, and he did not wish to fall behind in making an appearance from time to time on television. Cubbage, as a well-known "TV personality," was watched as much for himself on his programmes—indeed usually much more —as on account of the sometimes very relative celebrity of those caught up in the Cubbage net, persons whose popular fame was often far inferior to the interviewer's own. Shadbold would be a case in point.

A terse even derisive treatment of his subjects had brought Cubbage high renown, while he had also developed special techniques in dealing with individuals under examination. One of these forms of virtuosity was a flair for happening on unforeseen persons and unrehearsed incidents which would be abruptly introduced into a Cubbage programme with startling effect. Cubbage would pluck extempore dialogue, sometimes disturbingly expressed, from altogether alien sources which had an uncanny tendency to reveal themselves at hand. These were on the whole likely to turn out in one way or another highly embarrassing to whoever lay pinioned in Cubbage's clutches.

Shadbold was perfectly aware that some topic discordant to himself was bound to be launched in the course of the interview, but had earlier taken reassurance from the fact that his wife would also be present. Although he knew that she did not at all care for Cubbage she was, like himself, a practised hand in television performances, so that shock-treatment from the interviewer was unlikely to extract the least indiscretion from her. Owing to the comparative remoteness of the cottage no neighbours were sufficiently near easily to be drawn in. The worst Cubbage was likely to be able to lay hands on in the way of chance extras for his scenario was Mrs. Trout should Cubbage activities coincide with one of her "days." In such conjunctures with press or media Mrs. Trout, having herself once spoken on local radio regarding the brewing of dandelion wine, was scarcely less able to look after herself than Prudence Shadbold.

Cubbage's altogether unusual vanity, innate conviction that he and only he could possibly be right in settling any question whatsoever, was sufficiently overpowering to consign him to the very verges of sanity, a condition well adapted to putting on a good show from the impression conveyed that at any moment he might easily collapse into mental disorder of a serious kind. He delighted in interrupting and browbeating anyone not prepared to stand up to him. Such methods had caused little or no anxiety to Shadbold, whose own self-satisfaction was also considerable, nor were his manners specially polished. In short were incivility to become competitive Shadbold felt fully capable of giving a good account of himself, more especially as he was confident of possessing the superior intellectual equipment. To these weapons were added the ability and mettle of his wife. Now that he was to lose her support he began to feel a little less hardihood as to possible conflict.

The manner in which Cubbage had deeply offended Prudence Shadbold at the publisher's party at which the germ of the projected programme had come into existence was not known even in general bearing to her husband, but an immediate and acute antipathy had been at once conceived. Accustomed to carry his famous brusqueness of demeanour into private life (if he could be said to have any private life, the furthest extent of which being sometimes to be encountered at functions of that kind) Cubbage was easy enough to dislike. Nonetheless Shadbold, so far as having any sort of relationship with Cubbage were possible off the box, had got on passably well with him. He hoped to do so again in the more artificial interchange ahead of them.

11

Taking up the briefcase containing her notes for the first draft outline of *Culture-code of Samphire* Prudence Shadbold prepared to get into the car. Before doing so she once more recited the items her husband was charged to remember.

"And above all don't forget the saline washes for Lord Jim's feet."

"I'll break a jar of precious ointment over them."

"Do it on one of Mrs. Trout's days so that she can help hold him."

"Gentleman Brown has a touch of halitosis."

"He may be needing a pill."

"Where are those pills?"

"In the second drawer of my desk."

"Is the car running all right again?"

"The plugs have been seen to. It should get me as far as the Grighams' and back."

"Don't get murdered yourself."

"More likely die of starvation."

"And make sure Horace doesn't think he's the one in your book done in by Dreadful Trade."

Indicating that she could do the last on her head Prudence Shadbold kissed her husband, and drove off up the lane. Shadbold moved by easy stages towards his type-writer. He had slept badly the previous night. Pondering between half-past three and half-past five on Winterwade and his capabilities as a writer—the oddness that Winterwade should write such a bad novel and keep so good a diary—there had been moments when Shadbold had considered ringing up Jason Price to announce that he had changed his mind about the Diary, would after all like to have another look at it with a view to editing. If he did the editing he would undoubtedly retain a certain control, be able to suppress, at least effectively blur, all that was displeasing to himself. There could scarcely be anything more vexatious than the Isolde Upjohn incident. Then he remembered the war. Reading about contemporaries who had been in the army particularly irked him. Even the navy or RAF, unsympathetic as they might be, were for some reason more tolerable than the army in that respect. Still he now felt certain regrets as to unwillingness to face further decoding, had to remind himself what a labour that would have been. Undoubtedly a great deal of private interest had been lost, curiosity defeated by indolence and jealousy: a suitable subject for an allegorical picture.

Then the spectre of another publishing house accepting the Diary loomed beside Shadbold's bed, dispersed only by dawn glimmering through the curtains of the room, together with the realization that the manuscript was much more likely to be travelling (surface) to the Antipodes than to have found its way to another publisher. This was a quiet season in the book market, and he remembered there was little to look forward to in the work he was to review that morning; one, as it happened, written by a colleague of

Horace Grigham's and published by the University Press of their foundation: *Ealhwine the Coadjutor and Educational Reforms under Charlemagne*. Shadbold did not find the subject particularly tempting, but he wanted the money.

"Ealhwine, better known as Alcuin," typed Shadbold. "Educated at the cloister school of York under Archbishop Egbert . . ."

Having picked up what scraps he could on the subject of the Carlovingian liturgy and kindred matters from the book itself Shadbold decided to take a strong line about Charlemagne's educational policies, while at the same time trying to compose his own mind into a condition of receptivity suitable for undertaking a television interview the following day. Questions were always the same, answers from time to time needed discreet renovation, a touch of pointing up in regard to angles of emphasis. No doubt Alcuin (Ealhwine, if preferred), even if unrequired to deal with Rod Cubbage on television, had been under pressure from similar dualities of routine. Cubbage, intellectually speaking, was likely to be neither above nor below the cultural standards of his kind. At the same time—no doubt resembling those Carlovingian prelates Shadbold was now so vigorously castigating in his review—Cubbage was a prima donna of exceptionally peevish temperament to be carefully watched while in orbit. If properly handled there seemed no reason why he should not turn out a reasonably cooperative interrogator. That was provided Shadbold himself kept his head throughout the interview. The telephone bell rang.

"Hullo?"

"Can I speak to Mr. Shadbold?"

The voice, a woman's, was soft, appealing, somewhat

dowagerlike. Shadbold, unable to place its implications, judged caution best. He assumed a flat metallic tone.

"What name, please?"

"Mrs. Abdullah—but he won't know the name."

"I'll see if he's available."

Shadbold paused for a second or two with a hand over the mouthpiece to give an impression that he had been summoned to the telephone from a distant room in a spacious house. Still unable at all to place the speaker he played for safety with the manner of one interrupted while in deep intellectual concentration.

"Hullo?"

"Geoffrey . . ."

Shadbold's Christian name had not been in common usage since the memory of man. For a split second of horror he wondered if the speaker could be his first wife—quiescent in Californian exile for years and believed to be living with a retired disc-jockey in Palo Alto—but even she (unless having a row, which they usually were) had tended to address him as Geoff, rather than the latterly firmly established Shad. Besides this voice, though oddly evoking echoes of the past in the way Kay Conroy's might have done, had little in common with those stagey vocables, drawing-room-comedy-with-a-touch-of-cockney superimposed on old-fashioned RADA.

"Geoffrey . . ."

The name thus spoken, laden with seduction like waves of a once familiar scent recklessly sprayed on the body of a love-object, brought back a whole earlier style of speech; the way girls used to enunciate (if wishing to appeal) when Shadbold was young. Here again was the voice of The Twenties, faint on Shadbold's ear as the horns of elfland,

66

but still resolutely proclaiming the decade's clarion call that, even if by now Youth was battened down under the hatches, Pleasure was still inviolate at the helm.

"Who is it?"

Shadbold remained more than ever on his guard in putting the question, extending no more than the merest workaday amiability of tone to the other's cooing note.

"Isolde."

"Who?"

"Isolde."

"I still can't quite get the name."

"I used to be called Isolde Upjohn."

This last announcement was expressed with full force of Gertrude Lawrence / Tallulah Bankhead drawling articulation. After a moment of stupefaction Shadbold grasped the truth. Just preventing himself from saying "I thought you were dead" he was about to gain time by mumbling some noncommittal sentences indicative of sentiments genuinely complex enough, but found himself cut short by a torrent of explanation and request that needed full concentration of faculties to be transfused into the least sense, much less comprehended with any clarity.

". . . have only been back in England a few weeks . . . thought I must get into the country for a day or two . . . remembered coming to the Old Watermill Hotel on a rather idyllic weekend years and years ago with my American husband . . . the divine man who keeps it now happened to mention that you lived almost next door, Geoffrey . . . the *one* person I wanted to see . . . so many things to talk over . . . something you *must* do for me . . ."

Shadbold took hold of himself.

"This was Crowter?"

"Yes, Major Jock Crowter. Too sweet for words, as you must know as you live so near. I thought you'd probably turn up in the bar of such a lovely place, but as you didn't I got your number from Major Crowter and thought I'd look in on my way back to London."

"Yes, it would be nice to meet—"

"I'm starting at once . . . so will be with you in about twenty minutes . . . Major Crowter has given me the route . . ."

If there was one man on earth loathed by Shadbold that was Major (some said risen to no higher rank than captain) Jock Crowter, who managed the Old Watermill Hotel at some miles' distance from the cottage. This was the last straw. He disliked the pub as much as its manager. Crowter always behaved as if he were taking part in a quiz with Shadbold, and once when Prudence Shadbold had given Frieda Mutch, the Yorkshire detective-story writer, lunch at The Old Watermill when she had dropped in unexpectedly, there had been some sort of an altercation about Frieda Mutch's dog. Shadbold had sworn never to enter the place again.

"Perhaps you could give me luncheon . . ."

"The thing is, Isolde—"

"I might even stay the night if you've got a spare bedroom . . . No particular hurry to get back . . . I'd *love* to meet your wife . . ."

"Isolde, Prudence is away for a day or two—"

"Well, that's really better, isn't it? . . . though I would absolutely adore to see her some day . . . but if she's not there we'll be able to talk over old times without awkwardness, I mean . . . she'd have been a *child*, I gather, in those prehistoric times, wouldn't she? . . . madly young in my eyes even now . . . perhaps wasn't even born . . ."

"Isolde—"

"You're going to say you're like me . . . never have any lunch . . . one meal a day quite enough at our age . . ."

"It isn't that—"

"Anyway we can decide whether or not we want to eat when I'm with you . . . how ecstatic it's going to be . . . I can't wait, can you? . . ."

"What I was going to say—"

"If you do want to gnaw at some food I could cook it . . . I'm quite a good cook nowadays . . . does that surprise you, Geoffrey? . . . couldn't do more than boil an egg in the old Chelsea dump . . . now all sorts of exotic oriental dishes . . . I could cook yours at least . . . hardly take any nourishment myself these days . . . just peck at a speck like a sparrow . . ."

"Isolde—"

"Isn't it thrilling your being able to see me . . . there's something I particularly want to tell you . . . and ask you . . . I know it will all excite you no end . . ."

"I was going to say—"

"Don't bother . . . not worth wasting breath . . . I'll be with you in two seconds, Geoffrey . . ."

"Isolde, I ought to warn you. I've got a beard now. It's a fairly neat one, but white of course, and my hair's white too, what's left of it."

As she rang off he recognized her old laugh, now grown not only husky but close to raucousness. He hurried off to the bathroom to trim the beard, and changed his trousers, which dated back a long way.

69

12

Afterwards, weeks afterwards, Shadbold saw the second fatal blunder had now been committed. The first had been to have anything whatsoever to do with the Winterwade Diary. Once the truth of Isolde Upjohn's physical reincarnation had sunk into his consciousness as an established fact his first inclination had been, by a show of patent lack of enthusiasm, to prevent—at worst postpone—this invasion until such time as might allow due consideration of the probabilities her irruption might portend. That reaction on his part had been hopelessly inadequate. Her pertinacity should have been answered without hesitation by a statement that he was leaving the house at that very moment, and (like Captain Oates, thought Shadbold) could not say for certain when he would be returning. In retrospect he never quite decided why he had acted with such weakness and indecision. There had unquestionably been mitigating circumstances. Just as he had been curious to see the Winterwade Diary, he had been curious to set eyes again on an old flame. He was also prepared to admit to himself that he was not unwilling to exhibit to her gaze as presentable a façade as could reasonably be attained without too much effort. There seemed no obvious risk of ensnarement or obligation. He could recall nothing that a woman he had not seen for so long could possibly require of him; certainly nothing that would not be easy to refuse.

Shadbold had once asserted in a lighter moment to Jason Price (who was boasting of having had some woman in one night a superlative number of times) that he was himself still a comparative stranger in the corridors of impotence, but he had at once dismissed from his mind, whatever attractions Isolde Upjohn might retain, any question of attempting to achieve goals so keenly sought in the distant past. That resolution was made as much in the light of unforeseeable jeopardies of more kinds than one, in which any such fulfilment or attempt at fulfilment might land him, as on account of a grain of self-distrust. Besides he did not for a moment doubt that the evidently quite strong motivation of her visit was inspired not so much by pure affection, still less love, as desire to get something out of him. Notwithstanding effusive overtones that aim had been more or less admitted during the telephone conversation.

One thing at least had been clear to Shadbold, only too clear, while he attempted to define his own feelings in relation to what was not much less than a thunderbolt. Unlike the effect of the Winterwade Diary, this prospect of confrontation with Cynara (as Jason Price would certainly have schematized what lay ahead) had the very opposite effect to striking Shadbold sick from an old passion. In fact he could not imagine why only a few weeks ago Isolde Upjohn's trip to Paris with Winterwade had seemed so highly objectionable to himself. Now, thought Shadbold, the best to be hoped for was that this reunion should not too painfully resemble one of those encounters so chilling to the narrator's marrow that took place at the Princesse de Guermantes's last recorded party, nerving himself for some Toulouse-Lautrec *sous-maîtresse*, of whom the best to be said would be that she had the air of presiding over one of the better-class establishments.

13

The knock on the front-door was a noticeably light one, the discreet intimate tap of a true-love arriving for a clandestine assignation, its announcement designed to attract as little attention as consonant with gaining entry to the love-nest. More than ever uneasy Shadbold smoothed the few hairs of his head, gave a final jerk to the beard, moved forward to face this moment of truth.

"Geoffrey . . ."

"Isolde."

The shock was less than in anticipation. He saw at once that so far as personal appearance was in question—making due allowance for the fact that her age was only a few years short of his own—Isolde Upjohn was not merely as well preserved as might reasonably be hoped, but very well preserved indeed; in Jason Price's terms again a positive Dorian Gray of the female sex. Indeed for a split second Shadbold reconsidered earlier resolves; then discretion once more prevailed. She had kept her figure, dyed her hair with the utmost subtlety, dressed with the old mastery of current fashion, the raspberry trouser-suit seeming by no means out of place. To that extent Shadbold was aware of at least a small sense of relief. She looked perfectly all right, not only respectable, elegant as in the past, but positively affluent.

"Come in, Isolde, come in."

Remembering that decades before she had made a great hullabaloo in disallowing a kiss in a taxi passing through Sloane Square he had been uncertain whether a similar endearment launched by himself at this renewed meeting would be in the circumstances an appropriate gesture, even more a wise one. When, without pausing a moment, she herself kissed him on the lips, he caught a glimpse over her shoulder of a large blue Mercedes parked in the lane.

"But I love the beard. It gives just the right touch of careless distinction. How long have you had it, Geoffrey?"

"Oh, years now. You're looking very well yourself, Isolde."

Her comment reinforced the view that vital changes had taken place in mutual relationship. Nothing approaching approval of Shadbold's personal appearance had ever before been voiced by her, still less in the past had she condescended to the least suggestion of respect for anything he was doing or had done. If the exterior Isolde Upjohn remained relatively intact, drastic changes must have taken place within. Shadbold judged it best to play for time in ascertaining the object of the visit. Less than ever was he able to credit the violent emotions that had overcome him on reading of Winterwade's Paris trip with her. They had vanished now with the snows of The Twenties.

"Shall I make some coffee?"

"No, a scotch. A very mild one."

The fear at once struck him that she had become a drunk. Should he say there was no alcohol in the house, that for a period of time he had been forbidden by the doctor to drink, and, his wife away, stocks had not been renewed? Then he noticed a three-quarter-finished whisky bottle standing on the cupboard just in front of where Isolde Upjohn had stretched herself at full length on the sofa. At worst she might empty the bottle, after which he would assert no more was available nor anything else either. He poured out a pub-single.

"Lots of water," she said.

Shadbold complied generously in that respect, excusing himself from accompanying her at so early an hour in the morning. He was relieved to see that she sipped the scotch slowly, rather than gulping it down in dire need; then, setting the glass aside, seemed to forget about what remained there. Instead of revealing whatever was on her mind to provoke the visit she seemed disposed to reminisce about the past.

"Do you ever find youself in Chelsea now, Geoffrey?"

"Not often as it happens."

"You remember when you and I met in the King's Road?"

"Which time?"

He hoped she was not going to recall the Winterwade incident.

"We were both passing the Duke of York's Headquarters—the Duke of York's hindquarters as we used to call it in those days—coming from different directions, you on the way to see me, me going to the flat of some boring old lesbian who insisted on my having a drink with her. I'd much rather have come back to the flat and talked to you, but it couldn't be."

Shadbold, having no recollection whatsoever of any such

incident, suspected she recalled some similar occurrence with another of her young men, but he gave a nod and smile to allow the fragrant possibility of some such old regret. The objective was to get through all that had to be said and speed her on her way.

"What's been happening to you, Isolde, in all these long years?"

"You well may ask."

She sighed.

"How's it all been?"

Probably she needed just to get her life story off her chest to some one known to her in earlier days, would then go in peace.

"That was just what I wanted to talk about."

"You are still married—your husband was in oil, wasn't he?"

"God, no. Not to him. I've had three husbands since the one you're probably talking about—well, you could almost say four in a manner of speaking—and I've lived all over the place too."

"There's been time for a lot to happen."

Shadbold was aware that sounded sententious, but sententiousness seemed to offer the safest conversational atmosphere until the air had been cleared as to why she was present.

"I've been married twice myself," he added.

"Yes, but you've stuck to your writing. You've become a famous man of letters. I've just lived dangerously—tycoons, sheiks, shady politicians, *poules de luxe*, terrorists, straight criminals, heaven knows who else."

She sighed again; probably with good reason Shadbold thought. He was not at all sure where this was leading.

While appreciating being congratulated on intellectual integrity—the sort of bouquet that did not always come his way—he remained a little suspicious of that particular brand of compliment emanating from so unexpected a source. Then he made a fatal error of judgment. He had always supposed Isolde Upjohn's ability to express herself in the arts to be restricted to drawing. Such brief only very occasional communications he had ever received from her (invitations to bottle-parties and the like) had been all but illiterate. On that account he spoke thoughtlessly.

"You ought to write your memoirs."

Her reply was deeply disturbing.

"I have, Geoffrey."

"Indeed?"

"That's just what I wanted to talk about."

Shadbold shifted speedily into reverse.

"Of course just at the moment I understand publishers are very reluctant to take on memoirs, unless written by an ex–Prime Minister or someone like that. At least that's what my own publisher was saying the other day when I was talking about what was selling. His comment had nothing to do with anything that concerned myself. Personally I've never considered writing memoirs. They're a line I don't at all fancy."

"Mine are almost certainly going to be serialized in one of the Sunday papers."

"Which one?"

The answer—a journal not among the two or three more reputed—only a little reduced Shadbold's apprehension that she should find it necessary to inform him of this venture at all.

"That's very satisfactory then."

"The point is this, Geoffrey, that I'm sure I'll get them published as a book eventually, and the moment Major Crowter mentioned your name and said he'd often watched you on telly, I saw that what you must do is to write an Introduction to them. I got on the line to Humphrey at once, and he absolutely agreed that would be an excellent idea. Set them off to a good start."

Shadbold was so overcome with astonishment and disrelish at this proposal that he made no immediate attempt to answer. Something written by Isolde Upjohn, even ghosted for her, was an eventuality for which his mind was utterly unprepared. Doubtless taking silence to signify assent, she showed no expectation of a reply, rattling on in enlargement of her theme, again more than once quoting Humphrey, whoever he might be. Shadbold enquired on this last point.

"Humphrey helped me with the writing. He's a journalist. I'm sure you'll think he's done it very well. Humphrey says that the public like to read about how money is made and spent and lost. I've known a lot of people who did all that sort of thing. They were all right some of them, anyway in the places where I found them—a few very interesting and attractive, several rather nasty—and they seemed just the sort of people Humphrey was talking about."

"I see."

Shadbold felt a little better, at least a little safer. If the book was to be nothing more than a few sensational stories for the popular market about oil sheiks, high-class tarts, and the like, there was little to worry about.

"It's really very good reading some of it."

"I'm sure."

Shadbold doubted whether the stuff would get further

78

than a page or two in one issue of the Sunday rag she had named, if that; certainly never reach hard covers. Should some publisher prove mad enough to take it on Shadbold himself could always invent some reason for evading the desired Introduction.

"All the same, Geoffrey, I don't look on the sort of people I'm talking about now as anything like the best part of my life. Not at all. What I feel romantic about are those days when I lived in a garret, and used to draw for the glossy papers. Do you remember them, Geoffrey?"

"I do."

"And people like you would drop into my flat."

"Yes."

At that juncture another knock came on the front-door of the cottage, a knock quite unlike Isolde Upjohn's delicate tap. This time it was a loud hammering. Shadbold remembered that a local tree-surgeon had promised to look in one day in the near future to advise about a branch of the sycamore in the garden that had begun to show signs of threatening danger if brought down in a gale. This was probably the timberman arriving. He might be used as an additional excuse to cut short an unprofitable visit.

"I'll just go and see what this is."

Isolde Upjohn retrieved the scotch, finished it, put the glass far from her in a manner to show neither expectation of nor desire for a refill. Her face assumed a dreamy expression.

"There's something special I want to tell you, Geoffrey, when you come back."

She stood up, and began to examine the bookshelves.

14

Several large cars and vans had drawn up where the blue
Mercedes was parked in the lane. From these about half-a-
dozen persons, one or two bearded, dressed for the most
part in bright anoraks, were extracting and assembling
equipment of some sort from the vehicles. Among them
was a woman carrying a clip-board. On the doorstep stood
a clean-shaven man of forty-five or fifty wearing a dark suit
of slightly eccentric cut. He had elaborately "styled" hair, a
complexion that looked as if at one time or another the
whole of his face had been fearfully scalded with boiling
water, the demeanour of an actor playing a Shakespearian
tragic role. This was Rod Cubbage.

"We're a bit late, Shad. Had trouble with one of the
vans. But we're here now, and won't waste time."

He took Shadbold's hand, crushing the fingers in a dramatic grip, at the same time peering into his face with
an expression that might be registering either remorse or
rancour.

"But you were coming tomorrow, Rod."

Shadbold spoke in a manner to make as clear as possible that he was not only taken aback by the sudden intrusion of Cubbage and his crew, but extremely displeased.

"No, Shad, today."

"But we went into the whole question of which day of the week was most convenient to both of us."

"I know we did, Shad."

"And it was decided—"

"It was decided we came today."

"I'm certain—"

"You should write things down, Shad. It's the only way. Especially now you're getting older. Much safer. I've got a marvellous memory, quite phenomenal, nothing I miss, but I always write things down just for the record, at least I see my secretary does."

"Most certainly I write things down, Rod."

Cubbage ignored the statement.

"Come along, lads and lasses, come and meet Shad."

Shadbold all at once felt former tolerance of Cubbage vanish in a flash. Dislike not only equalled that expressed by his wife, but far exceeded hers. Nonetheless he recognized that further protestations would be a waste of time, the best to be hoped being to turn defeat in one direction into a form of victory in another. He allowed himself to be introduced to the crew, now standing round bearing their paraphernalia, and purported to welcome them into the house. The girl with the clip-board, grinning ferociously, attached herself to Cubbage, who at once began to give instructions right and left.

"Check up on the plugs, Sparks, and come along all of you. We'll have a run round these ruins, and see whether the pictures and furniture need some altering, as they probably will."

Cubbage and his retainers, followed closely by Shadbold, swept forward towards the sitting-room where Shadbold had left Isolde Upjohn. She had chosen a book from one of the shelves and was studying its pages closely. Shadbold saw it was *Beyond Narcissus* in her hand. She did not at first take any notice of the new arrivals in the room, then began to read aloud:

"A man who shoots himself for a woman is not necessarily more in love than one whose excitement at their first meeting is so great that he forgets to write down her telephone number."

She looked up and smiled.

"You know that's very true, Geoffrey. Don't you agree, all of you? Geoffrey wrote that because he knows about such things."

Assuming the air of one who had only just noticed this sudden influx of strangers she smiled graciously round.

"I'm afraid I didn't hear you come in. I was so lost in Geoffrey's wise and witty reflections. All the same don't you agree with Geoffrey in writing that sentence? I often found myself that it's impossible to guess the effect of love on certain men. Their temperaments are all so different."

Cubbage treated the question as rhetorical, anyway not requiring an answer from himself.

"Hullo, Mrs. Shadbold. I'm hoping to persuade you to embark on another of those arguments with me you're so fond of. They'll make splendid television when I'm interviewing your husband."

He held out his hand. Isolde Upjohn took it cordially, the warmth of her manner indicating that she forgave unconditionally his mistake in supposing she was Prudence Shadbold. Shadbold became angrier than ever. Not only was Cubbage's failure to remember what his wife looked like positively insulting after meeting her only a month or two before, but his whole demeanour was offensive in its familiarity. He was behaving as if he owned the place. At the same time Shadbold was still sufficiently master of himself to see, so far as dislodgment of a social encumbrance, that Cubbage's advent might be turned to even better advantage than the anticipated tree-surgeon.

"This is Rod Cubbage. Rod—Mrs. Abdullah. Mrs. Abdullah is an old friend of mine who found herself staying in a pub in this neighbourhood, and discovering I lived nearby dropped in to see me on her way home."

"Hullo, Mrs. Abdullah. I mistook you for Shad's Prudence. It's wives you expect to find in the house at this hour of the morning. I see such a lot of folk all the time that faces are bound to get misty however good your memory, as mine is."

"Pros was sorry she couldn't be here, Rod. She had to absent herself for a day or two in connexion with her own writing. As you remember, she's Proserpine Gunning, author of the famous detective novels."

Shadbold included Isolde Upjohn in this call to order. Cubbage grinned, making no comment.

"Rod Cubbage and his crew have come to do a television interview about me, Isolde. I thought it was going to be tomorrow, but it seems there's been some sort of a misunderstanding about dates, which of course I'll have to fall in with—so I'm afraid our pleasant little talk about old times will have to be terminated."

Even as he spoke the words Shadbold saw that getting

83

rid of Isolde Upjohn was going to be no easy matter. She could hardly have missed the point of being mistaken for a woman so very much younger than herself. Quite apart from a misconception highly favourable to her own looks she showed every sign of delight to have been given this opportunity of meeting Rod Cubbage.

"Oh, Mr. Cubbage, is it really you? Of course I recognized you at once, even so I could hardly believe my luck."

Cubbage smirked.

"I haven't been back in England very long, but I've already made a *necessity* of watching all your television interviews."

Shadbold interposed himself before Cubbage could attempt any answer.

"Mrs. Abdullah and I haven't seen each other for a number of years. As you've heard, she's not long arrived back from abroad. We've been having a brief word about the past—happy memories and as always some sad ones—and now I'm sure she'll have to be getting on her way. I'm really sorry, Isolde, that I should turn out to be quite so heavily engaged. For some reason the older one gets the less one seems able to escape every kind of professional commitment."

The fact that Cubbage was accustomed to a good deal of flattery, both from fans and those who regarded him as in one manner or another professionally useful to themselves, had by no means blunted in him a taste for adulation. He continued to smile in contented agreement with Isolde Upjohn's applause, at the same time evidently endeavouring to assess the practical value of this unstinted esteem. Well versed in taking the temperature of an audience, he

84

had already instinctively grasped from Shadbold's manner the existence of something more than willingness to divest himself of this visitor; the suspicion that she had already been showing herself an embarrassment to her host at once suggesting the sort of atmosphere in which Cubbage liked to conduct investigations.

"But an old friend of Shad's is just what we want. This couldn't have fallen out better, Mrs. Abdullah."

"How nice of you to say that, Mr. Cubbage."

"What I need most of all is someone to talk about Shad's early days, and you're the one to do it."

"Do you really think so?"

"I'd even suggested to Shad that someone like you ought to be present. He said he'd be only too glad to produce an old friend if he could, but there were scarcely any left. All he could offer was his wife. Will you stand in for Mrs. Shadbold then, Mrs. Abdullah? Naturally I thought Mrs. Shadbold was going to be here to take part in what I hoped would be a lively discussion, as she loves arguing, especially with me. But even Mrs. Shadbold wouldn't have been able to go as far back as you can."

If Isolde Upjohn felt this reference to her age somewhat negatived the earlier implied compliment she took that in her stride. In any case it was evident that after Cubbage's opening she had no other thought than to penetrate the programme. Her eyes gleamed at the prospect.

"What a marvellous idea. I'd absolutely love that. But don't call me Mrs. Abdullah. My name is Isolde. I used to be Isolde Upjohn, and some people thought I was a beauty a thousand years ago, though I don't expect you to believe that now. I've just written my Memoirs, so all those wonderful days in The Twenties are fresh in my mind. I can tell you all about them, most of all what Geoffrey was like then."

Cubbage pricked up his ears at the mention of Memoirs. "Who is Geoffrey?" he asked.

"It's my first name," said Shadbold curtly.

He could not fail to see the situation was becoming increasingly out of hand, and tried frantically to think of some means of checking its rapid career downhill.

"People always call me Shad nowadays, Isolde. Have for years. But look here, we can't involve you in all this TV business. You'll want to be getting along to wherever you're on your way to, see all sorts of people like myself you haven't seen for years. Anything to do with filming, as I'm sure you know, involves hours of boredom and hanging about."

"Of course I know that, Geoffrey. My second husband was in movies. There's nothing I enjoy more. I was given a test, and they said I could have been a star if I'd wanted. But Geoffrey—what a boost for my Memoirs. It's just what I need."

"This is all super," said Cubbage. "Don't be such a spoilsport, Shad. See some sense. Of course Isolde is going to appear. She'll be the making of the programme."

"I don't think I can allow this. I never agreed that I'd—"

"You told me how good you thought the Beverly-Baines programme I did, when we brought in the Chelsea Pensioner, and Simon got so cross. You said you'd never laughed so much. That's the beauty of the Cubbage programmes. Full of surprises. Isolde's sent from heaven."

"Yes, it will be divine, Geoffrey. Don't be silly. I'd love to do it, and I know I'll do it jolly well."

"I—"

"Now keep quiet, Shad. We've got exactly what I want in Isolde. I can see she's one of those natural TV artistes. I could tell the very moment she opened her mouth. With Isolde's help we'll shoot a stunning programme on you, Shad. How are things going, boys? We'll start business in this room here."

15

While the crew were setting up cameras and lights Shadbold's exasperated protests continued, Isolde Upjohn chattered unceasingly, Cubbage issued orders and bickered about technical details. Before Shadbold was properly aware what was taking place a three-cornered conversation was being filmed beneath the quartz-lights.

"Now as to Love in those days," said Cubbage. "Have you any comments you'd like to make about Love when you were a young man, Shad?"

Shadbold, who had been prepared for some such interrogation on that subject, had memorized a few clichés suitable to employ in answer, but by no means supposed they would have to be pronounced under the eye of Isolde Upjohn. He now gave an imitation of a man reflecting on the past.

"Well, Rod, it was an incomparable period for people being in love. Everybody one knew was always in love. My impression is that Love was a great deal more talked about than it is today. Nowadays, so far as I can gather, talk is chiefly about Sex."

"What do you think, Isolde?" asked Cubbage.

"What Geoffrey says is absolutely true, Rod. Geoffrey—really I can't learn to call him Shad, it seems so distant—used to declare he was in love with me, didn't you, Geoffrey?"

Shadbold raged inwardly.

"I suppose I was speaking no less than the truth, Isolde. Yes, I certainly was, but that didn't mean—"

"Now what didn't that mean, Shad?" rapped out Cubbage. "That's just what we want to know. What didn't it mean?"

His eyes protruded. His tone was that of a bullying counsel cross-examining in a criminal case of unusually degrading kind.

"Geoffrey is explaining that he and I weren't lovers in the physical sense. You must realize that, Rod. You belong to a younger generation, a freer one, and you don't altogether understand this perhaps. Geoffrey was trying to say that today people think Sex the only aim anyone has. Things were different then. The fact that we were not lovers in that way didn't make Geoffrey any less in love with me. That's true, Geoffrey, isn't it?"

"I agree I—"

Cubbage showed signs of finding too much unsatisfied Sex tedious.

"Tell us something about what Love was like when Sex did enter into it, Isolde. Make a few comments on that."

"I've talked a lot about Love in my Memoirs, Rod. You know Geoffrey mentioned that I'd written Memoirs. They're going to come out quite soon."

"No, you spoke of them, Isolde. It wasn't Shad. He hasn't talked about them yet. I hope he will in a moment. You tell us about them first."

"I remember now it was me mentioned them. I forgot that. What I mean is that Geoffrey can explain why I've written some of the things I have when I begin telling you about the Memoirs. Geoffrey can add enormously to the picture."

"We'll make him come clean, won't we, Isolde?"

Isolde Upjohn ignored Cubbage's facetious tone. Instead of concurring in a mood of derision she assumed an expression to suggest profound emotion. She now addressed herself specifically to Shadbold.

"I want to talk about an old friend of yours, Geoffrey."

"Which one?"

Shadbold's heart sank to the furthest depths yet achieved. He hoped against hope the name would not be the one he feared most of all. She dropped her voice almost to a whisper.

"Cedric Winterwade."

"Ah, yes?"

This was not to be borne. He fumbled for a defensive plan.

"The writer."

"I recall he wrote one book."

"You remember dear Cedric?"

"Of course."

"Of course you do. Your greatest friend."

"One of them."

Cubbage had plainly never heard of Cedric Winterwade, but again from Shadbold's demeanour he could sense embarrassment in the offing.

"Tell us about this great friend of yours, Shad. What did Cedric Winterwade do?"

"He was in the City."

"One of these tycoons?"

"No, just worked in a stockbroker's office."

"Oh, but Geoffrey, say something about Cedric's writing. He was author of a wonderful book called *The Welsons of Omdurman Terrace.* I've read it over and over again."

"I was coming to that," said Shadbold.

He tried to think of the most concise summary for disposing of the whole Winterwade subject without at the same time appearing at all hostile either to the man or his book.

"Poor Cedric," said Isolde Upjohn.

"Poor Cedric," echoed Shadbold.

Winterwade's misfortunes might offer the key. He must somehow gain time, attempt to dominate the situation.

"Why was he poor Cedric?" asked Cubbage.

"He lost his life in the war."

"Oh, I see. Sad."

Cubbage spoke without any strong sense of conviction.

"You remember how sweet Cedric was, Geoffrey?"

"Very nice man."

"You and Cedric were always about together."

"I suppose we were at one time."

"But not when you came to see me."

"No, just that once as I recall, when you met us both in the street."

Shadbold wondered what would come next. He braced himself.

"Just that once."

"Yes."

"Those were lovely days, Geoffrey."

"They seem a long time ago."

"Tell us more about this guy Winterwade. What sort of a love-life did he have?"

Shadbold tried to seize the initiative.

"Much what we all did in those days. I don't think there was anything particularly exceptional about Winterwade's. He got married comparatively young. A very pretty girl, I seem to remember."

"Oh, but there was something exceptional about Cedric's love-life," said Isolde Upjohn. "Something you don't know about, Geoffrey. That's one of the things I want to speak of. It meant so much to me, and it affects you too, Geoffrey."

"This sounds exciting," said Cubbage.

"Geoffrey—Cedric was in love with me."

Shadbold had begun to feel more desperate than ever. Isolde Upjohn's next words were spoken to convey increasingly a note of impregnable holiness.

"Geoffrey—Cedric was deeply in love with me."

"So many men were, Isolde."

"But Cedric especially."

"I did hear a rumour later."

"But not at the time. No one knew at the time. Cedric's love for me was always kept secret."

"It was?"

Shadbold spoke with polite interest.

"Now this is good stuff," said Cubbage. "You and Winterwade were in love with the same girl, Shad. It was bitter rivalry even though you may not have known it. That's a good situation. Capable of a lot of development."

Isolde Upjohn was quick to put any such supposition right.

92

"Oh, no, indeed it wasn't like that, Rod. Geoffrey never had an inkling about Cedric, did you, Geoffrey? Cedric always impressed that on me, that Geoffrey didn't know, Cedric felt badly about your not knowing, Geoffrey."

Shadbold, who had hitherto managed to maintain an outward calm, was unable to hide all irritation at this condescending attitude towards himself on the part of Winterwade.

"I can't think why he should have felt badly, as you call it. Who Cedric was or was not in love with was no business of mine."

"Ah, you pretend that now, Shad," said Cubbage. "I bet you did have a suspicion at the time. I bet you did."

Shadbold ignored him.

"Cedric had some pretty strange girlfriends at one moment or another," he said. "I certainly remember that about him."

"So Cedric Winterwade had strange girlfriends, did he?" said Cubbage, temporarily losing the scent. "Tell us about some of them. Are you implying there was a touch of kinkiness? What form did the strangeness take? Won't you put a few of Winterwade's girlfriends into the context of the period? That might be intriguing."

With a dismissive movement of her hand Isolde Upjohn crushed Cubbage's unguarded divergence from the essential matter under discussion.

"Cedric and I were lovers," she said simply.

"You were?" said Cubbage, now in triumph. "Well, what—"

Isolde Upjohn turned away from him, once more confronting Shadbold as the only person who mattered in this revelation.

93

"For a *very* short time."

This was it. The Paris trip was coming out. Shadbold cursed himself for being unable to say that he knew all about the weekend when she and Winterwade had been lovers, including knowledge of what a fiasco that incident had been. Why had he botched such an opportunity? Yet to mention the Diary would be to reveal the whole story of its suppression by himself.

"Does that surprise you, Geoffrey?"

"Nothing surprises me at the age I've reached, Isolde."

"But it would have then, Geoffrey?"

"I dare say it might."

Cubbage was altogether unable to grasp lights and shades of the story. He made no pretence of understanding its bearing at all.

"Why should it have surprised you, Shad? If all the chaps you say were honeypotting round Isolde, surely that was just what to expect?"

The two of them had put him out of his depth, made him uncertain what line to embark on next, which questions now best to cause embarrassment. Isolde Upjohn's general attitude had thoroughly unsettled Cubbage.

"Cedric thought it was going behind Geoffrey's back."

"But, Isolde, what did it matter if Cedric was going behind my back, if he really thought that? You never gave me any reason to suppose that being in love with you conferred rights on me as regards to your choice of lovers. Why should it?"

"All's fair in love and war," interjected Cubbage, speaking as if he had just originated that proposition.

"It mattered to Cedric, Geoffrey."

"So you two weren't lovers?" said Cubbage.

The fact had now come to him as unassailable.

"Now that's interesting," he went on. "How do you account for such a thing? I expect you would have been lovers these days. What you were saying about Sex, I mean. How did it feel not being lovers?"

Shadbold, still addressing himself to Isolde Upjohn, disregarded Cubbage's now random shots.

"Cedric was over-sensitive about such matters."

"Dear Cedric. Perhaps he was. That was one of the things I found so sweet about him. But, Geoffrey, you did like Cedric's book, didn't you?"

Cubbage went off on a new line.

"Yes, tell us something about Winterwade's novel. I expect you both appear in it. First books—I gather this was his only one—are usually autobiographical. Especially if you were his best friend, and he was in love with Isolde. It's ten to one you're both there. Some revealing stuff, I expect."

Shadbold spoke categorically this time, conscious he was swimming in very deep water.

"*The Welsons of Omdurman Terrace* was not in the least autobiographical in any direct sense, though it may have expressed certain literary and other inclinations of its author, even moral preoccupations in relation to persons known to him. It was a work by no means without all interest. I remember giving it a favourable review at the time."

"Omdurman Terrace?" reflected Cubbage. "Now that's a name evocative of old imperialist days. Would you like to say something of the sunset of imperialism, Shad? Did

Cedric Winterwade reflect any of those aspects of the contemporary scene? It's an emotive picture you might like to spread yourself on."

Shadbold saw that Cubbage's inability to stick to the point could in the end offer hope of salvation, but was afraid that if he grasped too obviously at this straw lightly extended, Isolde Upjohn would bring him to heel again by return to the subject of her love for Winterwade. It might be better first to dispose of the novel.

"I'm not sure what I'd think if I re-read *The Welsons* today. By that I mean I'm uncertain how far Cedric's style of writing may have stood up to modern changes of fashion."

The measured tone of this statement was intended to suggest approval of literary criticism as a return to serious matters after fairly wild speculations about Love, Sex, all that. Grigham was unlikely to watch the programme when it appeared. If he did Shadbold would deal *ad hoc* with whatever apparent contradictions of his own that might seem open to objection on Grigham's part in relation to Winterwade's novel. Cubbage, making from his own point of view something of a recovery, must have thought quite enough literary criticism had been voiced to be readily digestible.

"That's enough about Cedric Winterwade's book. Let's get back to his sex-life. Now, Isolde, would you like to say a word about Cedric Winterwade as a lover? Any special memories you'd like to recall?"

"Oh, yes, Rod. The time when Cedric and I went to Paris together."

"You went to Paris?"

"In the spring."

"That's the season for Paris."

96

"The trees were coming out in the Luxembourg Gardens."

Cubbage looked uncertain.

"Don't you mean the Champs Elysées, Isolde? That's where people usually see them coming out."

"We stayed in a little hotel in the Latin Quarter."

"Somewhere Cedric Winterwade knew about?"

"Cedric had been told of the hotel by Geoffrey. Oh, Geoffrey, how grateful we were. That's one of the reasons you must write the Introduction to my Memoirs. Say how you first heard about The Bouguereau, how you wanted your friend to know about it too. And also to proclaim to the world what a great writer Cedric would have become if he hadn't been killed. That trip to Paris was the most perfect experience of my life."

Shadbold, who had by then got himself pretty well under control again, suddenly felt an anger more than he could master. For the moment he ceased to care where what he said might lead.

"Look, Isolde, you musn't mind my saying this, but apparently Cedric talked about that Paris trip with you to a man he and I both knew, and years after Cedric was dead that man passed on to me some of the things Cedric had said."

Cubbage made delighted gestures of approval.

"I didn't know at the time that Cedric must have been with you," Shadbold continued. "I see now it can only have been the same occasion. It was at The Bouguereau just the moment you said. Apparently Cedric thought the girl he was with—that is you—had really persuaded him to take her there because she wanted to meet another man in Paris."

In supposing this method of using the Winterwade Diary for disingenuous ends would discompose Isolde Upjohn no misjudgment could have been greater on Shadbold's part. She was only amazed at such naivety.

"But of course that was when Cedric went to Paris with me. I had to meet that first husband of mine there, and hadn't any money for the journey. Cedric was the only way."

"Couldn't your first husband have sent you the money?"

"He had."

"Then why did you have to be taken by Cedric?"

"Because I'd spent the money, Geoffrey. What do you think?"

Shadbold took a second or two to recover.

"I had to get to Paris, otherwise that awful man probably wouldn't have married me."

"But why Cedric?" asked Cubbage.

"I'd always had quite a soft spot for him, though it was thinking about him years after showed me what I really felt."

"Cedric must have guessed something of the sort was on about another man," said Shadbold.

"Oh, I'm sure he did. He was very intuitive in that sort of way. That was one of the things that were so nice about him. He didn't ask any questions."

"But then Cedric told this same man when he was dishing up the Paris trip—well, you mustn't mind my saying this, Isolde—said that the night hadn't been at all successful."

Shadbold realized that he was speaking with a recklessness that might easily lead to unthinkable complications.

"The night with Cedric? But it was *dreadful*. Both

nights were—for each of us—and the afternoon worst of all. That didn't make it any less a wonderful experience."

"Now that's an interesting point—" began Cubbage.

She interrupted him, concentrating on Shadbold.

"But, Geoffrey, what I really wanted you to tell me is how Cedric died in the war. What actually happened? Which front was he on? I'm sure he was heroic, but I want to know where and when and in what way."

"I really have no idea. I never heard."

Shadbold felt utterly dazed.

"You never found out?"

"No."

"But surely you enquired?"

"There was so much going on then."

"You can find out now. You must find out. Will you promise to get to work on that now, Geoffrey, and let me know?"

"But I've absolutely no idea what Cedric was doing in the army. I don't even know if he was an officer or in the ranks. All I heard was that he was dead. It's all such a long time ago."

"I know it's a long time ago, Geoffrey, but I must know. How can I do that? Geoffrey, you can help me. I did so love Cedric."

"Cut," said Cubbage. "Good stuff some of that. There's lots more for us to talk about."

16

In retrospect Shadbold could remember little else of the day beyond the glare of the quartz-lights, repeated snap of the clapper-board accompanied by the words "Take one," pauses during reloadings of the cameras, sharp exchanges between Cubbage and the crew, the grinning face of the girl-assistant in the background, the same subjects churned up over and over again with Isolde Upjohn, until no embarrassing opinion or grotesque revelation remained unconfessed by him.

An interlude for lunch, by adding a new dimension of horror to what he was enduring, remained more clearly in his mind. Disregarding a plea that he should stay at home and snatch a snack by himself Isolde Upjohn, backed up by Cubbage, insisted that Shadbold should accompany them to the Old Watermill Hotel, where, as ever, Major Jock Crowter was in the bar. Promoting the goodwill of the house was Major Crowter's main contribution to the business, more onerous duties like cooking, accounting, general management, falling to the lot of Mrs. Crowter, an energetic Amazonian blonde with metallic mustard-coloured hair, to be sighted from time to time through the hatch that gave on to the kitchen. Crowter, probably in his early sixties, tall, weatherbeaten, aggressive side-whiskers, check jacket with leather-patched sleeves, cavalry twill trousers, would when appropriate sport a deerstalker ornamented with fishing-flies. He greeted Isolde Upjohn with uneasy exuberance.

"Back so soon, Mrs. Abdullah? This is very good news. And Mr. Shadbold. Good morning, sir. Haven't seen you in donkeys' years. Torn yourself away from your books at last, have you? It's been a long time since we've had the pleasure."

If any rancour remained as to the matter of Frieda Mutch's dog (there had been some unpleasantness about the bill too) all was forgiven and forgotten in Crowter's delight in finding The Old Watermill was not only to enjoy the patronage of a camera-crew but a camera-crew under the hand of Rod Cubbage. Cubbage turned out to be the object of something not far from worship in Crowter's eyes. In fact Cubbage's presence in The Old Watermill that day seemed to be the highspot of Crowter's life from the way in which he was behaving. Cubbage too was in his element in such appreciative company.

"This is a real treat for us, Mr. Cubbage. Something out of the way to meet you in the flesh. What with fishing, sailing, golf, the pony club, weekend adultery, it's usually a case of nothing new from this end as the monkey said to the toilet-roll, but today you've made our day, Mr. Cubbage. I never thought I'd wring you by the hand. I can't be too grateful, Mr. Shadbold, for you bringing your friends along."

Crowter made a tremendous bustle with drinks, then more drinks. During lunch Shadbold found he could scarcely eat anything. When it was time to return to the cottage Cubbage tried to invite Crowter back with them to take part in the afternoon's shooting, but Isolde Upjohn stepped in to veto that. In any case some all-powerful but shrouded force—probably Mrs. Crowter—appeared to forbid Crowter from moving further afield than the pub's premises that afternoon. While the question seemed to hang in the balance Shadbold, putting forward a strong but unspoken moral opposition, was preparing himself, had there been no other intervention, for a downright refusal to have Crowter in the house.

By the end of that day Shadbold had admitted to an admiration for *The Welsons of Omdurman Terrace*, agreed that Winterwade had died a hero's death that he himself envied, promised to do his best to find out the circumstances in which Winterwade's heroic end had taken place. At moments it seemed his torments would never cease. The only thing he still retained as his own was the secret that the Diary existed. Somehow that never came out. Isolde Upjohn had dominated the proceedings throughout, not least dominated Rod Cubbage himself. Shadbold had no recollection how finally he had managed to eject them from the house. When at last Cubbage and his retainers drove away, the blue Mercedes had been part of the motorcade.

Shadbold spent most of the following day in bed. He would have remained all day there, so much had the previous twenty-four hours worn him out, had not Lord Jim and Gentleman Brown made so great a hubbub outside his bedroom that he could get no rest until he had fed them.

Usually at odds with one another, the cats now united in reproaching him for disrupting their routine in this detested manner. Shadbold took the opportunity of having something to eat himself. In an attempt to soothe his nerves he gave Gentleman Brown a pill, and rather superficially washed Lord Jim's paws in a solution of salt. This was in some degree to put himself in a slightly less vulnerable position on his wife's return. In other respects he scarcely reflected at all as to what the next move would best be.

17

By the time Prudence Shadbold drove up to the cottage he had made up his mind to attempt recovery of the Winterwade Diary from Jason Price, but paralysis of the will prevented any coherent plan, much less active steps to achieve that end. Shadbold was equally undecided how best to disclose the various happenings that had taken place in the house during his wife's absence in a manner to create a minimum of astonishment and indignation in her mind. That these elements must find a place there was inevitable, but so far as possible the story ought to be presented in the most advantageous light for toning down its many undeniable follies and irresolutions. He lamented incessantly that in the first instance he had not recommended the Diary's publication, while adding that he was himself too busy to undertake decipherment and editing. In that manner he would have possessed a weapon to keep Isolde Upjohn at least temporarily at bay, probably by shifting her activities on to whoever had shown the hardihood to accept the job. He could have refused to discuss Winterwade at all until the Diary had appeared, anything like rapid publication being extremely improbable.

So far as offering explanations to his wife was concerned the collision turned out less imminent than he had feared. Prudence Shadbold's first impulse on arriving home was to recount at length the tribulations she had herself suffered in consequence of staying with the Grighams. Apart from physical discomforts endured—they had been many including having to hear a performance by Janice Grigham on the French horn—a serious professional impediment was now put in her way. Much of what Shadbold had predicted as to Horace Grigham's probable reaction to the plot of the new Proserpine Gunning novel turned out all too well substantiated. Grigham had shown himself thoroughly difficult; indeed raised what might be insuperable objections to the whole orientation of the narrative.

Prudence Shadbold indicated how she had at first dropped only tentative hints as to matters in her book that might require sensitive handling, were somewhat similar characters or events known to her hosts as having any parallel at Grigham's university. Then, coming out in the open, she had outlined in comparative detail the narrative of *Culture-code of Samphire.* This plain speaking had caused dismay. Earlier foreshadowings of the plot had not been at all fully understood by the Grighams. There were, so it turned out, many resemblances in the projected story to persons and events connected with their professional and social circle. In addition to that Horace Grigham displayed an obstinate conviction that the murdered professor was intended to be a caricature of himself on the part of his ex-wife. In fact after listening to what amounted to a synopsis of the novel he made the strongest representations that it should not be published in anything like its present form.

"Horace even had the cheek to hint that if it came out he might be obliged to—those were his actual words—seek legal advice."

Prudence Shadbold poured out another drink for herself.

"The fact is I shall have to rewrite the whole book."

"Campus life turned out just what your most vivid flights of fancy had pictured?"

"And worse."

"I did warn you, Pros."

"All the most sinister and perverse acts I'd thought up are the daily life of this academic backwater. At least that's according to Horace. They only seem to have stopped short of murder, and murder appears by no means ruled out in the near future. It will probably take place on publication day just to prove the point against me."

"Of course Horace may have invented the whole thing from spite."

"He was certainly unnecessarily difficult about some of the scenes I sketched in. I only told him out of pure kindness of heart. We'd once been married, and I didn't want to ruffle him too much. He went so far as to say that I'd written the whole book to be disagreeable about him."

"I told you not to tamper with Horace in a detective novel. He belongs to the realm of science-fiction."

"I'd just forgotten what Horace was like, how impossible he can be. I tried to explain that any chance resemblances to him were not my fault. These pictures stick in the subconscious after you've been husband and wife, then come out when you're just novelist and novel. Horace couldn't see it that way. He has no imagination whatever of course."

"Horace sounds a great nuisance."

"He was awful."

"And Janice?"

Shadbold wanted to delay as long as possible the tale he had himself to tell.

"I nearly emulated the house-guests at Glencoe. But tell me more about this man Cedric Winterwade whose diary you were reading for Jason Price. Why is he of such interest? All you said was that it was no good and you used to think him a shit."

"Why on earth do you want to know about Winterwade?"

"Horace asked me what you had been working on lately. I think from the way he put it he rather hoped you'd retired for good from the active scene these days. I said on the contrary you were always very busy. The most recent thing you had been doing had been reading the diary of a contemporary of yours called Cedric Winterwade for a publisher. That was the only job you'd had lately I could remember. I wanted to make clear to Horace that you were still hard at it. Hearing the name Winterwade had an absolutely atomic effect on Horace. What's it all about?"

"You told Horace I'd been reading the Winterwade Diary?"

"Yes, why not? It wasn't a secret, was it? If so you never mentioned the fact to me."

"I particularly didn't want Horace to find out about the Diary."

"Then why didn't you warn me? How was I to know that?"

"I never supposed the subject would crop up between you and Horace. I didn't realize you'd even taken in Winterwade's name when the manuscript was in the house."

"But what does it matter if I did?"

"Too complicated to explain. Horace thinks the novel Winterwade wrote years ago might be useful in his teaching."

"So he said. Horace went on for ever about Winterwade and his novel, the name of which I can't remember. Was it something about the battle of Omdurman? You know what a bore Horace can be on the subject of books that have caught his attention, especially when he's going to inflict them on his pupils. It's because he's a thwarted writer himself. I thought he'd never stop. In the end I switched off and didn't listen."

"I know that when it comes to talking all night Heraclitus wasn't in it with Horace, but what did you actually say about me and Winterwade?"

"Only that he was a man you used to come across occasionally years ago and always thought rather a shit."

"You told Horace that?"

"What are you getting at? Was it a carefully guarded secret that Winterwade was a shit? It's something pretty public as a rule when that's said about somebody. Why are you going on like this, Shad?"

"Just tell me word for word what Horace's emotions were when he learnt from you that Winterwade had kept a diary, and I'd seen it."

"He was carried away. It was the one moment when Horace ceased nagging about *Culture-code of Samphire*. Instead of being purely destructive about my book he suddenly brightened up and showed a little interest in something. Is he contemplating writing a critical work on Winterwade's novel about Omdurman?"

"Something of the sort is swilling about in what Horace uses for a mind."

"Or lectures? Come to think of it lectures are more what it sounded like."

"But did Horace show any signs of wanting to get in touch with me about the Diary?"

"No. Definitely not. I suggested that, though I told him I was pretty sure you'd sent it back as of no interest whatever. Horace said he thought you'd prefer not to be bothered about Winterwade—very unlike Horace to consider anyone else's feelings in that way—so he said he was going to get in touch with Jason Price himself. Price seems to be a friend of that colleague of Horace's who wrote the book on Charlemagne or whatever it was you were complaining about having to review when I left you here for the Grighams'."

"Oh God!"

"Did you forget to review it?"

"No, it's not that, it's Horace sticking his nose into Price's business."

"I can't make out what you're in such a stew over. If the Diary is being sent round to publishers there can't be any particular secret about it. When it was in the house you said it wasn't of the least interest."

"The Diary wasn't of any interest from your point of view. It just happens to be awkward for me that Horace has got to know about my adverse judgment of its merits."

"Well don't let's go on talking about Winterwade's Diary any more, or about Horace and Janice, whom I've seen enough of to last for the rest of my life. How did the Cubbage interview go? Was dear old Rod his usual charming self? The one thing that kept me going at the Grighams' was the thought that at least I was missing Cubbage."

Shadbold took a deep breath. He knew he must make a vigorous effort to master this latest contingency to arise complicating his predicament, if possible repair some of the damage resulting from so lamentable a failure on his own part to come out on top in the matter of the Cubbage programme.

18

The story ended at last after much interruption and questioning on the part of Prudence Shadbold. There was a long pause. Shadbold knew that he had failed in an endeavour to pass over his recent experiences as scarcely worth recounting. He tried to think of some new light in which to set them which might enhance their triviality. His wife began again.

"What I don't understand—I still can't understand, Shad—is who this woman Mrs. Abdullah really is. Why should she suddenly call on you after all these years? In many ways what you've been telling me simply doesn't make sense."

"I've explained all I know, Pros. Let me repeat it. Mrs. Abdullah used to be called Isolde Upjohn. She was regarded as quite a beauty in her day. That's a long time ago, as you say. I just happened to know her. She was the sort of little piece who knew thousands of men. Men swarmed in her flat. It was always assumed she was kept by somebody, but I never heard who that was. Then she got married and disappeared from London."

"Do you mean she was more or less a tart?"

"No, no. Of course not. Nothing like that. She used to do a bit of modelling, and I think once drew little pictures for a fashion article."

"Did you have an affair with her? You never told me."

"I've already explained I never had an affair with her. In fact at the time I never knew anyone who did have an affair with her, though it was universally agreed that somebody must have been paying the rent."

"You're certain you never had an affair with her?"

"Nothing I'm more certain about."

"But you were chasing after her in those days?"

"Only as dozens of men were. I never had a chance. I just took her out to dinner once or twice, and used sometimes to look in on her flat, if I happened to be passing and had nothing better to do."

"How squalid."

"It wasn't an indictable offence."

"What happened to her after she got married?"

"That's just what I've been trying to explain. I only know what she told me while she was here. First she married an oilman, then apparently had a series of other husbands—tycoons, Arabs, journalists, movie people, God knows who else. She seems to have got round quite a lot."

"Did she have any children?"

"She didn't mention any. That may come in the Memoirs, which she said were going to appear in some low-grade Sunday paper."

"Is that what she wants you to do an Introduction to?"

"Only if they are published in book-form. I'll be able to get out of that if necessary. It was just difficult to say outright that I wouldn't do the Introduction."

"So she can write?"

"The Memoirs seem to have been more or less ghosted by a man she calls Humphrey."

"Who is Humphrey?"

"I have no idea."

"Is she living with him?"

"I shouldn't wonder."

"Have you read her Memoirs?"

"Of course not."

"She might have brought them with her."

"She didn't. I only heard about them for the first time when she told Cubbage during the interview. She'd only been here five minutes when Cubbage and his crew turned up."

"So she talked about the Memoirs on television?"

"Yes, as I told you, but I'll get out of it."

"How?"

"I'll find a way."

"But you agreed on the programme?"

"I didn't absolutely say in so many words whether I would or not. She just assumed I would. She will probably never find a publisher."

"So by implication you consented to write an Introduction to a book of Memoirs you'd never set eyes on?"

"Cubbage changed the subject at that moment, later I couldn't get back to what had been said and clarify my own position. I meant to bring it up again, but Cubbage began running on about a whole lot of other matters I had to keep my head about."

"It doesn't sound as if you kept your head at all."

"Cubbage will probably cut most of that out anyway."

"Oh, no, he won't. It sounds to me like a frame up. Why should Cubbage have arrived on the wrong day? That's pretty suspicious in itself."

"Nothing suspicious about it. Just sheer stupidity on Cubbage's part."

"He'd probably fixed up every detail with this woman."

"But I tell you they'd obviously never met before. She's seen him on television, but when he first came into the room he thought she was you."

"Me? But she's about a century older. I never heard such a thing. Besides Cubbage knows me perfectly well. Knows how much I dislike him. He must just have been trying to be insulting."

"I told Cubbage not to be a fool. The fact remains he didn't know her."

"Probably arranged it all through an agent. And what I can't understand in your story is why you didn't send her about her business in the first instance, far less allow her to horn in on a programme that was supposed to be about you."

"It wasn't as easy as all that. I'd have been far more able to cope if you'd been there, Pros. I said at the time that you were choosing an awkward moment to go away. You could probably have seen her off with the utmost ease. Your absence was a great pity, indeed a disaster."

"And then why does everyone want to talk about this man Cedric Winterwade? I can't think why you never told me about him, or suggested that I should read his novel. Was he madly attractive? From what you say about Mrs. Abdullah, or whatever she's called, he must have bowled her over pretty well. She seems to have been crazy about him, running on all the time about Winterwade when the interview was meant to be with yourself. You'd better put Mrs. Abdullah in touch with Horace, so that he and she can drool over Winterwade together."

Shadbold sighed. There was another long pause. Then Prudence Shadbold began all over again. The saga of the Cubbage shooting had once more to be rehashed.

19

A comparative lull fell on the Shadbold household during the month or six weeks preceding the release of the interview in the series. Lord Jim and Gentleman Brown settled down again, the one no longer requiring attention to his paws, the other recovering from breath that caused offence. Mrs. Trout went on a coach-tour holiday. Meanwhile the programme was gloomily awaited by both the Shadbolds, though for somewhat different reasons. During the period of suspense the atmosphere could not be called good.

Things became vastly worse after the screening. In fact during the three or four days that followed Prudence Shadbold was too angry even to discuss the matter. At the same time, whatever additional scars inflicted by the actual showing of the interview, reprobation of her husband's manner of conducting himself was very slightly lessened by fiercely renewed antagonism towards Cubbage taking its place. Shadbold no longer needed to be permanently on his guard against surprise attacks. Interludes of shared hatred for Cubbage united husband and wife.

The programme had been edited in a manner to exclude

almost all material not actively displeasing, at best highly irritating, to the Shadbolds. Indeed the abrasive nature of the interview made a strong impression on those who watched it by the way in which a very different "image" of Shadbold was presented from that disseminated by himself now for several decades, most of all from that which in anticipation he had hoped to promulgate. A substantial fan-mail flowed in. Acquaintances wrote to say how keenly they had been entertained by hitherto unguessed sides of his character, most of them contriving to insert a small personal barb however slight. Strangers were impressed by the devotion with which he had never forgotten an old love and an old friend. All praised the part played by Isolde Upjohn; many wanted to know more about Cedric Winterwade. In the face of ingenious cutting and editing Shadbold's efforts to soft-pedal both those aspects of his past life failed utterly.

One of these fan-letters (no address, postmarked Hull) was destroyed by Shadbold as soon as its contents had been absorbed. After expressing the customary enthusiasm for the programme the writer of the letter, a woman, added: "You don't remember me I don't expect and I'm not going to sign any name but there was a girl you once knew called Bunty Meadows and if that name rings a bell it will be because there was a spot of trouble. That's the reason I'm writing because I never knew before that Cedric Winterwade was a friend of yours. Well I thought you ought to know how bloody well he behaved about that business though I had not been out with him for a long time after it blew up. You see I must have been one of the strange girlfriends he had that you talked about on the telly. He found me crying at a party and I told him what it was and he said he'd do something, sell his car or raise a pound or two somehow if it came to that and I was in a jam. Then that night it turned out a false alarm but bloody good of him. Thought you'd like to know as he was such a friend. Just had my sixth grandchild."

Nothing further had been heard by Shadbold of Isolde Upjohn. He had no idea where she was staying, not even whether in London or the country. For a time he lived in permanent dread that she might reappear at The Old Watermill, every incoming telephone call setting off a throb of apprehension. Matters other than Shadbold's Introduction to her Memoirs must be occupying her attention. By the time the shooting had come to an end the hold she had developed over Rod Cubbage was so powerful that Shadbold even speculated on the possibility, one not to be dismissed out of hand, that she might establish herself on the strength of the interview more or less permanently as a "television personality."

During this immediately post-screening period Shadbold, after dealing as best he could with the fan-mail, which occupied some time, nerved himself to take a positive move in order to ascertain the whereabouts of the Winterwade Diary. He did that by ringing up Jason Price, from whom he had heard nothing for a long time, nor seen in The Garrick on several trips to London. Price turned out to be undertaking an extended business visit to the U.S. Other members of the firm to whom Shadbold talked knew nothing of the Diary—essentially Price's private quarry— and in any case Shadbold was unwilling to involve a lot of new people in what from his own point of view was already

118

an undesirably complex situation; one likely to be worsened rather than improved by widening interest in its convolutions.

Pending Price's return Shadbold tried to occupy himself with odds and ends of work, or such matters as rather tedious correspondence in which the Alcuin review had landed him; but he knew he would have no peace of mind until the whereabouts of the Diary was revealed, enabling him to make fresh dispositions as to his own attitude towards it, ones that had no need to be kept secret. He had been sticking press-cuttings about the Cubbage interview into his book, trying to cheer himself by looking back through some of the old ones evoked by *Beyond Narcissus*, when his wife half-opened the door, speaking without entering the room.

"Crowter is outside. He wants a word with you."

"Crowter of The Old Watermill?"

"He's the only one so far as I know."

"What does he want?"

"I've no idea."

"Can't you get rid of him?"

"Look, I don't want to spend all the morning talking to Crowter, nor to you for that matter. I'm still trying to revise *Samphire* in such a way that it will satisfy that zombie Horace. It isn't all that easy. I'm determined not to lose the best bits. It takes time. So as Crowter wants to see you it's you who'd better see him."

"Bugger Crowter, and bugger Horace too."

Prudence Shadbold withdrew, Shadbold closed the press-cutting album. There was always the possibility that Isolde Upjohn had returned, and sent Crowter over with

119

some sort of message. That only occurred to Shadbold after a moment or two's thought. It disturbed him. He found Crowter had already infiltrated the house, was in fact reading a newspaper he had found in the hall. When Shadbold appeared Crowter's habitual expression of cunning intensified, demeanour that might at any moment turn to cringing or bullying according to which best suited the occasion.

"What can I do for you, Major Crowter?"

Shadbold's pointedly discouraging tone did not in the least conceal lack of trust in Crowter to the length of an inch. That reception in no way inhibited Crowter's synthetic mine-host geniality in portable form for outpatients.

"We've been hoping you'd drop in again, Mr. Shadbold, and I'd be able to tell you how much we all enjoyed your appearance on the Rod Cubbage programme. That's by no means the only reason why I wanted to see you. There's something in addition you're going to get very excited about. But let me say it was first-rate entertainment—you and Mrs. Abdullah and Rod, as he asked me to call him— one of those better class of items, instead of that eternal pop-music that gets me down day after day."

Crowter stopped speaking. He took Shadbold by the arm.

"Which way shall we go, Mr. Shadbold?"

"Can't you tell me here, I'm—"

"It's rather a long story, Mr. Shadbold, and I'm not sure it's one Mrs. Shadbold ought to hear, because I know I don't want to have it come to the ears of my own wife, but I guarantee from what you said on the programme that it's just the news you've been awaiting for years. With business in prospect at The Old Watermill I thought I might not have another chance for a month, and in any case there was the question of getting you on your own, which might have been difficult, though the wife's usually fully occupied. What I mean is I'd have been over before now if there'd been a spare moment. It was a case of no-can-do day after day. That's why I jumped into the car when the decks were reasonably clear. Let's sit here, and I'll tell my tale."

Seeing no chance of ridding himself of Crowter without hearing at least some of the story, whatever it was, Shadbold, resuming his own seat in front of the typewriter, pointed to a hard chair. He refused the cigarette offered by Crowter, in no hurry to reveal his secrets.

"When I told Mrs. Abdullah you lived in this neighbourhood I never guessed she'd know you, especially after being out of England for so long. And I guessed even less that I'd be watching her and you on television only a few weeks later. But what really got me stirred up was that both of you should have known my old comrade-in-arms Cedric Winterwade."

Shadbold winced. Crowter put a finger to his lips in a dramatic gesture to enjoin silence.

"You won't forget what I said about the wife?"

Shadbold nodded. He could not have conceived that yet one more eventuality should have taken so distasteful a course as that Crowter should have served with Winterwade in the army. At the same time at least one problem might thereby be solved. Crowter shook his head from side to side in mock remorse.

"What got me, Mr. Shadbold, was that you promised the lady you'd leave no stone unturned to find out how Cedric Winterwade died, when she said she'd give anything in the world to learn that. Of course I'd have told Mrs. Abdullah the whole story while she was staying with us if I'd known Cedric had been such a close friend of hers—she made that very clear, didn't she, the way people do these days—but the name never came up. She wouldn't have minded. I could tell that from the way she talked. When I heard how she felt, not to mention how you yourself felt, I thought the best thing to do was to come along and see you quick as I could. Then, as I said we were all so busy I hadn't a jiffy to call me own. You don't know when you'll be seeing Mrs. Abdullah?"

"No, I don't."

"Anyway you can pass it all on to her when you do next meet up with her, which will be pretty soon, I expect. What I wanted to say was that would you mention she left a scarf with us. I meant to tell her when she came over with Rod Cubbage on that day, but it slipped my memory, there was so much going on then, and I'm not sure of her address to send it."

"Neither am I."

"Well I've no doubt she'll be back soon as she seemed to enjoy her visit."

"Look, you were going to tell me how Winterwade died."

Few subjects, as such, less activated Shadbold's curiosity, but he judged some knowedge of the circumstances likely to prove useful—if not essential—in prevention of further persecution of himself in that particular field. By cutting matters short he hoped at the same time to dislodge Crow-ter, who now seemed to be settling down to devoting the whole morning to a lengthy narrative. Any expectation of abridgement was dissipated at once by Crowter himself.

"When I got my commission towards the end of the war, Mr. Shadbold, I was sent to India. Didn't particularly want to go, but there it was. Long story which I won't go into. That was how it all began. I was in a Transit Camp in Bombay. It was there I ran across Cedric Winterwade. He was quite a bit older than me. All the same he only had two pips, and we chummed up for some reason, though he was what you might call a bit of a loner, intellectual type, just as you are yourself, Mr. Shadbold."

"You were in the same regiment?"

Shadbold knew nothing of the army, and cared less. All he wanted was to be told the bare facts of Winterwade's death, those related as briefly as convenient. There seemed no way of extracting that from Crowter.

"Not a bit of it. Cedric was General Service or the I Corps, don't remember which. He was going to be posted as Cipher Officer to some formation. Then it was a case of snafu—situation-normal-a-fuck-up if you'll excuse an army expression—and he was kept hanging about for weeks just as I was. In the end I got sent to Burma, and was wounded."

Crowter made the motion of patting his body, presum-ably indicating the anatomical area that had suffered, at the same time offering another cigarette.

"So Winterwade was killed in Burma?"

"No, not at all. I'm coming to that. Now I expect you've heard of Grant Road, Mr. Shadbold?"

"In London?"

"No, no, in Bombay."

Crowter was amused at the question.

"I haven't. What about Grant Road?"

"Now I thought everyone had heard of Grant Road in Bombay. That does surprise me in a man of your great knowledge as I'm aware from quiz-programmes."

Shadbold saw no end to this rigmarole if he had to follow Winterwade's military career from point to point in every theatre of war until he lost his life.

"Didn't mean to imply anything by that, Mr. Shadbold, but Grant Road's the famous Red Light district of Bombay. Thought everybody knew that."

"What's Grant Road got to do with Winterwade?"

"You're quite right. What indeed? Especially considering the quiet sort of guy Cedric was. You know he never particularly liked tarts. What he did like was getting about and seeing things. That was why he enjoyed going round with me. By that time, hanging about in that bloody Transit Camp, I'd learnt quite a bit about Bombay. Some of it pretty spicy I can tell you, Mr. Shadbold. That's why I was so interested when you and Mrs. Abdullah talked about the book Cedric had written. I can see now that Cedric was going to write a book about our nights out together. I never guessed that at the time."

Shadbold looked at his watch. Crowter made no change of pace. If anything he decreased speed.

"You'll see now why I wanted to tell you this when the missus wasn't about. I was young then. Needed a night on the tiles once in a way. If Grant Road was my objective Cedric would come along with me until I'd settled into a comfortable billet, then he'd peel off back to quarters. Never seemed to be panting for a Donald Duck. Had to be careful of course."

"You mean of catching something?"

"Catching the APM."

"An Indian form of VD?"

Shadbold was at sea.

"Not only Indian and nearly as bad. Worse sometimes. Assistant-Provost-Marshal. Military Police wallah. Snoop about trying to catch you out for being what they call improperly dressed, or going somewhere you didn't ought. Grant Road and neighbourhood was out of bounds. If you went you had to keep an eye out for the APM. What Cedric liked were the exotic girls looking as if they were behind prison bars. Then he'd laugh about the brass beds with knobs on, and the pictures of King Edward VII and Queen Alexandra at their Coronation. Cedric would talk for ever about that sort of thing. Seemed to keep him going in the army."

Crowter mused on that. Shadbold recognized potential Winterwade material for the Diary, regretting for a moment that in spite of distaste for military life he had not pressed on towards the end to read about Grant Road and the like. Crowter came to again.

"Cedric and I were cruising along there one night when we sighted the APM and his merry men. You can believe me we about-turned in double-quick time. Took separate ways as best tactics for evasive action. Passing one of the little shacks where the girls give you the one-two a dark-eyed floozie saw a bloke was being chased by the APM, and beckoned me to pop inside and hide under her skirt, which

I can assure you I did forthwith before you could say Jawaharlal Nehru."

Shadbold felt he was approaching the end of his tether.

"Major Crowter, what I am anxious to know about is Cedric Winterwade's death. For God's sake tell me that, not about your own sex-life, which if I may say so is no concern of mine."

"Quite right, Mr. Shadbold. I appreciate that. I'm sorry to have had to intrude it, especially as it turned out that the naughty girl didn't regard it as any concern of hers either. I found the last out to my cost. The next thing I knew was that I was waking up in the side-alley of a street quite a step away from Grant Road feeling as if I'd washed down my dinner the night before with a pint of Strontium 90. It was morning. I fumbled in my pocket. They'd taken every bloody thing. Hadn't a cent to my name, not even my pocket handkerchief and the packet of french letters I'd thought fit to add to my basic equipment. You can take it from a man who's had many a hangover in his day, Mr. Shadbold, that I've never felt worse, not even when the odd lump of Japanese mortar bomb hit me in Burma."

"What about Winterwade?"

"Poor old Cedric was even less lucky than myself."

"Why?"

Crowter was silent for a moment. He gazed at Shadbold. Then he spoke.

"Cedric was found in another alley miles away from the one I woke up in. They rigged it so it looked as if he'd been run over. Perhaps he had. That's easy enough the way they drive."

"Dead?"

126

"I'm afraid so, Mr. Shadbold."

"It was all hushed up?"

"Never heard what was said about Cedric. I had enough to do getting myself out of the shit, if you'll pardon describing my difficulties that way. Luckily the posting came along just at that moment, so there was a certain amount of least said soonest mended all round. But it was a sad end for a good type. Worst of it was he was only going to have a look-see. That was why I got such a lot from your programme, Mr. Shadbold. When I found out Cedric wrote books that explained it all about him to me."

Shadbold rose from before the typewriter. He held out his hand, at the same time making some pretence at a smile.

"Thanks for telling me all this, Major Crowter. I'm very glad to hear about the circumstances. As you remarked yourself, poor old Cedric."

"I knew you'd want to know the truth about an old friend, even though the story's a sad one. I felt sure of that because of all you said yourself on telly about how much Cedric's friendship meant to you. I often think of old Cedric and that night in Grant Road. I often think of Grant Road anyway. I had some times there in spite of everything. Well, I can't grumble. It's been an interesting life. No doubt about that. You'll tell Mrs. Abdullah about the scarf, won't you? Better use your discretion about the rest of what I've been saying."

"If I should see her."

"Just one thing more, Mr. Shadbold."

"Yes?"

"Cedric found he'd come out without any money that night, and as he'd said he'd stand me dinner, I'd lent him twenty rupees. Call it one pound fifty-pence in post-inflation currency, though of course it represented a lot more in the purchasing power of the pound in those days. I don't know whether as an old friend you wouldn't like to make that amount good in memory of Cedric?"

Crowter's eyes had narrowed, gone a shade watery, at thought of this possibility. Shadbold, coming to a quick decision, put a hand in his pocket. The comparatively small outlay represented payment for a story that had been in the end worth hearing. At least he had not been asked to make up the difference that thirty shillings had been worth at the time of Winterwade's death. He found three 50p coins, and handed them over.

"Now that's handsome of you, Mr. Shadbold. It's what Cedric would have done himself if things had been the other way round."

Crowter stood up.

"Don't forget us altogether at The Old Watermill. You ought to see some of the types we get nowadays. You might like to write about them. Served a rum-and-Coca-Cola to a young lady with pink hair sticking out all over her head in spikes last week. But to tell the truth chicks like that are the exception in the bar. It's the old fishing crowd as a rule, and we're always glad to see them—and you and Mrs. Shadbold, not to mention friends of yours like Rod Cubbage or Mrs. Abdullah, if they're looking in on you again."

Shadbold went as far as the front-door to make sure Crowter left the house.

"Things don't look too good in the Middle East to my way of thinking."

"No," said Shadbold. "They don't."

As Crowter made for his car he began to sing:

> *"I love Gaddafi,*
> *A bonny brown Gaddafi,*
> *He's as brown as the . . ."*

The final words of the verse, with their comparison, were lost as he slammed the car's door, and drove away up the lane.

20

The strong sense of relief felt by Shadbold in learning of the circumstances of Winterwade's passing were to some considerable extent based on consolation that there had been no question of charging a machine-gun nest nor carrying a wounded comrade to safety under fire. Over and beyond that alleviation was satisfaction in possession of the truth. How exactly this first-hand information might be put to best use was not immediately obvious. At the same time there was no doubt as to its eventual value. Properly presented even to Shadbold's own wife, for example, the story would to some extent justify lack of enthusiasm for Winterwade as an acquaintance, making up for former inability to produce any concrete unfavourable criticism as to Winterwade's manner of life. The shadiness of the Grant Road background might even provide some sort of offset in the case of renewed trouble from Isolde Upjohn. That was less to be built on.

Another effect of Crowter's visit was that Shadbold felt reduced urgency in seeking out the whereabouts of the Winterwade Diary. He gave up efforts to get into touch with Jason Price. He was conscious that at last he himself held a moderately useful card. For Price, too, he prepared a special version of the story, and was about to deliver it when quite by chance he ran into him at The Garrick. Price was rather apologetic. He began to explain that he had not contacted Shadbold on return from America because almost at once he had himself been plunged into exceptional business affairs that had been occupying all his time. What had happened, he explained, was that he had moved to another publishing house, where settling in had not allowed a moment to take up the threads of former connexions in his old firm.

"It's a change that had been on the cards for some time, Shad. No point in talking about it before the *fait accompli*. Won't make any difference to our seeing each other. In fact I was going to get hold of you as soon as one or two things were a bit clearer in my new office. Something's taken place there that is going to interest you a lot."

"What I really wanted to know, Jason, is what happened to the Winterwade Diary that you gave me to read, and I sent back with a fairly unenthusiastic report. You probably acted on it, returned the manuscript to whoever sent it. I've sometimes wondered whether I judged Winterwade rather harshly. If you've still got it, or have a note of its whereabouts, I wouldn't mind another glance through."

"Of course you want to know that. I was coming on to Winterwade. I can't too much regret that I wasn't here to see the Cubbage programme, which everyone has been telling me about. You know I managed to get an absolutely wrong impression about how you felt towards Winterwade himself. Do you remember I had a notion once of republishing *The Welsons of Omdurman Terrace?* You were against that. I must say on re-reading the novel I agreed with you up to the hilt. I suppose from what I've been told about your appearance on the Cubbage programme that you too re-read the book, and changed your mind the other way."

"Various things did make me revise my own view of Winterwade and his writing."

"But of course they did, Shad. I've been hearing about all that too. But what you won't know is that there's now a considerable interest in *The Welsons of Omdurman Terrace* in the teaching world. My new firm has quite a flourishing educational side, and there's an EngLit professor at one of the redbrick universities who's been keen on it. You wouldn't know about him, but he's called Grigham. He's going to approach Winterwade from an entirely new angle."

"I do know about Grigham as a matter of fact."

"That's one thing. Much more important from your point of view is that the first manuscript I found on my desk at my new job was that of the Memoirs of the lady who made such a lively contribution to your programme. There has been so much to do that I haven't had time to read them yet—they've been ghosted, I gather, and may be going to appear in one of the Sunday papers—but the agent who sent them says that you're very anxious to do an Introduction to them."

Shadbold felt rather unsteady, indeed shakier than he perhaps had ever felt in his life before.

"You say you haven't read them yet?"

"Only cast an eye. Not greatly impressed to tell the truth, but an Introduction by yourself might turn the scale, especially as you're so keen. I gather Winterwade played an important part in Mrs. Abdullah's—is that the name?—early life, as you did too. That's why you were anxious to do the Introduction. I wanted to talk about all that with you. Are you lunching here?"

"You haven't told me yet where the Diary is. Have you still got it?"

"Unfortunately not. It went back to the London-based Australian journalist who sent it to me in the first place. I made enquiries from him apropos of this new development, and he said he'd returned it to Australia. I asked him to find out if we could have another look at it—funny that you should have had the same idea, Shad—and he called me up yesterday to say that Winterwade's son had destroyed it as unsaleable. Didn't want it cluttering up the house. Pity, perhaps."

"Yes," said Shadbold. "A pity. Do you know I'm not feeling very well, Jason. Not like talking business at the moment. In fact I think I'll cut out lunch, and go back to the country this afternoon."

21

G. F. H. Shadbold's memorial service was held in one of the City churches, though Shadbold had no particular associations with the City nor for that matter with churches. Considering the cold of the winter day, attendance could be called good. Jason Price, suitably enough, pronounced what he himself styled the panegyric. He was agreed to have done that pretty well.

Price emphasized that Shadbold had been what he called a Man of the Twenties, though Shadbold had in fact come in only for the latter part of that decade. This gave opportunity for bringing up one of Price's favourite themes, the points of resemblance between The Twenties and The Nineties, and, in supporting this theory by quotation of some of the dedicatory verses at the beginning of John Davidson's *Earl Lavender*, he was even able to draw certain parallels with his listeners' own epoch. Like most persons who have gained access to a pulpit Price was determined not to abandon that vantage point until he had stated a fair number of his own prejudices as well as Shadbold's better qualities:

"Though our eyes turn ever waveward,
Where our sun is well-nigh set;
Though our Century totters graveward,
We may laugh a little yet.

Oh! our age-end style perplexes
All our elders time has tamed;
On our sleeves we wear our sexes,
Our diseases, unashamed."

This stanza gave Price just the opening he needed for developing his motif, although, in fact, Shadbold seems in the end to have found laughter provided an inadequate mitigation. Price managed to speak for quite a long time before closing (in a manner Ophelia might have approved) with the final recurrent stanza:

"Though our thoughts turn ever Doomwards,
Though our sun is well-nigh set;
Though our Century totters tombwards,
We may laugh a little yet."

Prudence Shadbold, who had always laid stress on her own matter-of-factness in the face of mortality, was no doubt consciously got up as for skiing, but as usual—especially in the case of writers and by no means excluding lifelong homosexual writers—several female friends were deporting themselves as Shadbold's widow; a kind of self-imposed moral suttee that is in its way a handsome tribute. All except one of these forlornly arrayed ladies were easily identifiable, most of them fairly well habituated to that role. This unrecognized figure, belonging more or less to

Shadbold's own age-group, had evidently been a beauty in days gone by. There was still an elegance about her which caused several persons who had been in the congregation to enquire on the way out who she could have been.

Jason Price, who lingered for some little time afterwards at the door of the church rather as if he had been widowed himself, explained that she was called Mrs. Abdullah. He recalled that she had been heroine of the celebrated Cubbage programme about Shadbold, adding that his own new firm had somewhat reluctantly turned down her Memoirs only a short time before as being of not quite sufficient interest to promise any great sale.

"Looking at her in church just now," said Price, "I was reminded of that line in one of Wilde's plays to the effect that women kneel so divinely."